Joel C. Harris

Little Mr. Thimblefinger and his Queer Country

what the children saw and heard there

Joel C. Harris

Little Mr. Thimblefinger and his Queer Country
what the children saw and heard there

ISBN/EAN: 9783337227876

Printed in Europe, USA, Canada, Australia, Japan

Cover: Foto ©Andreas Hilbeck / pixelio.de

More available books at **www.hansebooks.com**

LITTLE MR. THIMBLEFINGER
AND HIS QUEER COUNTRY

What the Children Saw and Heard there

BY

JOEL CHANDLER HARRIS
AUTHOR OF "UNCLE REMUS," ETC.

ILLUSTRATED BY OLIVER HERFORD

BOSTON AND NEW YORK
HOUGHTON, MIFFLIN AND COMPANY
The Riverside Press, Cambridge
1894

A LITTLE NOTE TO A LITTLE BOOK.

THE stories that follow belong to three categories. Some of them were gathered from the negroes, but were not embodied in the tales of Uncle Remus, because I was not sure they were negro stories; some are Middle Georgia folklore stories, and no doubt belong to England; and some are merely inventions.

They were all written in the midst of daily work on a morning newspaper, — a fact that will account in some measure for their crude setting.

J. C. H.

WEST END, ATLANTA, GA

CONTENTS.

LIST OF ILLUSTRATIONS.

LITTLE MR. THIMBLEFINGER AND HIS QUEER COUNTRY.

I.

THE GRANDMOTHER OF THE DOLLS.

ONCE upon a time there lived on a plantation, in the very middle of Middle Georgia, a little girl and a little boy and their negro nurse. The little girl's name was Sweetest Susan. That was the name her mother gave her when she was a baby, and she was so good-tempered that everybody continued to call her Sweetest Susan when she grew older. She was seven years old. The little boy's name was Buster John. That was the name his father had given him. Buster John was eight. The nurse's name was Drusilla, and she was twelve. Drusilla was called a nurse, but that was just a habit people had. She was more of a child than either Sweetest Susan or Buster John, but she was very much larger. She was their playmate — their companion, and a capital one she made.

Sweetest Susan had black hair and dark eyes like her father, while Buster John had golden hair and brown eyes like his mother. As for Drusilla, she was as black as the old black cat, and always in a good humor, except when she pretended to be angry. Sweetest Susan had wonderful dark eyes that made her face very serious except when she laughed, but she was as full of fun as Buster John, who was always in some sort of mischief that did nobody any harm.

These children were not afraid of anything. They scorned to run from horses, or cows, or dogs. They were born on the big plantation, and they spent the greater part of the day out of doors, save when the weather was very cold or very wet. They had no desire to stay in the house, except when they were compelled to go to bed, and a great many times they fretted a little because they thought bedtime came too soon.

Sweetest Susan had a great many dolls, and she was very fond of them. She had a China Doll, a Jip-jap Doll, a Rag Doll, a Rubber Doll, a White Doll, a Brown Doll, and a Black Doll.

Sometimes she and Drusilla would play with the Dolls out in the yard, and sometimes Buster John would join them when he had nothing better to do. But every evening Sweetest Susan and Drusilla would carry the Dolls into the bedroom and place them side by side against the wall. Sweetest Susan wanted them placed there, she said, so she could see her children the last thing at night and the first thing in the morning.

But one night Sweetest Susan went to bed crying, and this was so unusual that Drusilla forgot to put the Dolls in their places. Sweetest Susan's feelings were hurt. She had not been very good, and her mother had called her Naughty Susan instead of Sweetest Susan. Buster John, in the next room, wanted to know what the matter was, but Sweetest Susan wouldn't tell him, and neither would she tell Drusilla. After a while Sweetest Susan's mother came in and kissed her. That helped her some, but she lay awake ever so long sobbing a little and thinking how she must do so as not to be called Naughty Susan.

Drusilla lay on a pallet near Sweetest Susan's bed, but, for a wonder, Drusilla lay awake too. She said nothing, but she was not snoring, and

Sweetest Susan could see the whites of her eyes shining. The fire that had been kindled on the hearth so as to give a light (for the weather was not cold) flickered and flared, and little blue flames crept about over the sputtering pine-knot, jumping off into the air and then jumping back. The blue flames flickered and danced and crept about so, and caused such a commotion among the shadows that were running about the room and trying to hide themselves behind the chairs and in the corners, that the big brass andirons seemed to be alive.

While Sweetest Susan was lying there watching the shadows and wondering when Drusilla would go to sleep, she heard a voice call out, —

"Oh, dear! I believe I 've got smut all over my frock again!"

It was the queerest little voice that ever was heard. It had a tinkling sound, such as Susan had often made when she tied her mother's gold thimble to a string and struck it with a knitting-needle. Just as she was wondering where it came from, a little old woman stepped from behind one of the andirons and shook the ashes from her dress.

"I think I'd better stay at home," said the little old woman, "if I can't come down the chimney without getting smut all over my frock. I wonder where Mr. Thimblefinger is?"

"Oh, I'm here," exclaimed another tinkling voice from the fireplace, "but I'm not coming in. They are not asleep, and, even if they were, I see the big Black Cat in that chair there."

"Much I care!" cried the little old woman snappishly. "I'll call you when I want you."

Then she went around the room where Sweetest Susan's Dolls were scattered, and looked at each one as it lay asleep. Then she shook her head and sighed.

"They look as if they were tired, poor things!" she said. "And no wonder! I expect they have been pulled and hauled about and dragged around from pillar to post since I was here last."

Then the little old woman touched the Dolls with her cane, one by one. Each Doll called out as it was touched, —

"Is that you, Granny?"

And to each one she replied : —

> "Roser, roser, rise !
> And rib and rub your eyes !"

Sweetest Susan was not at all alarmed. She felt as if she had been expecting something of the kind. The Dolls arose and ranged themselves in front of the fireplace — all except the Rag Doll.

"Where's Rag-Tag?" inquired the little old woman anxiously.

"Here I am, Granny!" replied the Rag Doll. "I'm lame in one leg and I can't walk with the other, and my arm's out of joint."

"Tut! tut!" said the little old woman. "How can you be lame in your legs when there's no bone in them? How can your arm be out of joint when there's no joint? Get up!"

Rag-Tag rolled out of the corner and tumbled across the floor, heels over head.

"Now, then," said the little old woman, opening her satchel, "what can I do for you?"

"She's pulled all my hair out!" whispered the China Doll.

"She's mashed my nose flat!" cried the Jip-jap Doll.

"She's put one of my eyes out!" whined the Brown Doll.

"She's put chalk all over me!" blubbered the Black Doll.

"She has n't hurt me!" exclaimed the Rubber Doll.

"She's made a hole in my back, and the sawdust is all running out!" whined Rag-Tag.

"I'll attend to you first, before you bleed to death," said the little old woman, frowning. Then she rapped on the floor with her cane and cried out: —

> "Long-Legged Spinner,
> Come earn your dinner!"

While Sweetest Susan was wondering what this meant, she saw a big Black Spider swing down from the ceiling and hang, dangling close to the little old woman's face. Its little eyes sparkled like coals of fire, and its hairy mouth worked as if it were chewing something. Sweetest Susan shivered as she looked at it, but she did n't scream.

"A thimbleful of fresh cobwebs, Long-Legged Spinner!" said the little old woman, in a businesslike way.

Then the big Black Spider moved his legs faster than a cat can wink her eyes, and in a few seconds the fresh cobwebs were spun.

"That is very nice," said the little old woman. "Here's a fat Bluebottle for you."

The big Black Spider seized the Fly and ran nimbly to the ceiling again. The Fly buzzed and buzzed in a pitiful way, and Sweetest Susan thought to herself, "Oh, what should I do if that was poor me!"

Then the little old woman hunted in her satchel until she found a piece of mutton suet, and with this and the fresh cobwebs she quickly stopped the hole in Rag-Tag's back. This done, she went around and doctored each one. She glued more hair on the China Doll. She fixed the nose of the Jip-jap Doll. She gave a new blue eye to the Brown Doll.

"There!" she exclaimed when she had finished, "I think you look a little more like yourself now. But you would look a great deal better if you had any clothes fit to wear. Now pay attention! What is the name of this horrible giantess that drags you about and beats you so?"

"It's no giantess, Granny," replied Rag-Tag. "It's a little girl, and sometimes she's very, very good."

"Hush!" cried the little old woman. "Speak when you are spoken to."

"She *is* a giantess, Granny," said the Brown Doll. "She's taller than that chair yonder."

"Where is she now?" the little old woman asked fiercely.

"She's asleep in the bed, Granny," said the Brown Doll.

"Pinch her good, Granny!" cried the Wax Doll. "Put out her eyes!"

"Scratch her, Granny! Pull out her hair!" pleaded the Brown Doll.

"Bump her head against the wall, Granny! Mash her nose!" exclaimed the Jip-jap Doll.

The Rag-Tag Doll said not a word.

All this time the little old woman was searching in her satchel for something, and Sweetest Susan began to get frightened.

"I've come off without my specs," said the little old woman, "and I can't see a stiver with such a light as this."

Just then the big Black Cat that had been sleeping quietly in a chair rose and stretched himself and gaped, showing his long white teeth. He jumped to the floor and walked back and forth purring and rubbing against the little old woman in a friendly way.

"Get out! You'll push me over," she cried. "Oh, will you go away? I'll stick you with my needle! I certainly will! Keep your long tail out of my face! Oh, how can I see to do anything? Will you go away? I'll hit you as sure as I am standing here!"

"Don't," said the big Black Cat, stopping and looking straight at the little old woman. "Don't you know it brings bad luck to hit a black cat?"

"If I hit you, you'll feel it," cried the little old woman.

"Stop," exclaimed the big Black Cat. "I know what you are here for. Do you see my eyes? They are as green as grass. Do you see my teeth? They are as strong as iron. Do you see my claws? They are as sharp as needles. If I look at you hard you'll shiver; if I bite you you'll squall; if I scratch you you'll bleed."

The Grandmother of the Dolls looked at the big Black Cat long and hard.

"Do I know you?" she asked.

"I know you," replied the Black Cat.

"What is your name?" she asked.

" Billy-Billy Blackfoot."

" It is time for you to go hunting," she said. She wanted to get him out of the room.

" I have found what I was hunting for," said Billy-Billy Blackfoot.

" There's a rat gnawing in the pantry."

" He'll be fatter when I catch him."

" There's a piece of cheese in the dining-room."

" It won't spoil until I eat it."

" There's a pan of milk in the kitchen."

" It won't turn sour till I drink it."

" There's catnip in the garden."

" It will grow till I want it."

The Grandmother of the Dolls then made a cross-mark on the carpet and waved her cane in the air. This was done to put a spell on Billy-Billy Blackfoot, but before the spell could work Billy-Billy made a circle by chasing his tail around. Then he glared at the little old woman and slowly closed one eye. This was too much. The Grandmother of the Dolls seized her cane and made a furious attack on Billy-Billy Blackfoot, but he leaped nimbly out of the way and the cane fell with a whack on the bald head of the Brown Doll.

At this there was a tremendous uproar. The Brown Doll screamed: "Murder!" Billy-Billy Blackfoot's tail swelled to twice its natural size; the hair-brush fell on the floor; the dustpan rattled; the shovel and tongs staggered out from the chimney-corner and rolled over on the hearth; the Dolls scrambled and scurried under the bed, and the little old woman whisked up the chimney like a spark from a burning log.

When Sweetest Susan raised up in bed to look around she saw Drusilla sitting on her pallet rubbing her eyes, but Billy-Billy Blackfoot was sitting by the fireplace washing his face as quietly as if nothing had happened. At first it seemed to Sweetest Susan that it had all been a dream, but presently she heard a small voice that came down the chimney:

"Mr. Thimblefinger! Mr. Thimblefinger! It is nine minutes after twelve." There was a pause, and then the small voice sounded farther away, like an echo, "Nine minutes and two seconds after twelve!"

II.

MR. THIMBLEFINGER'S QUEER COUNTRY.

THE next morning Sweetest Susan was awake early. She wanted very much to turn over and go to sleep again, for her eyes were heavy and her body was tired. But the moment she remembered the wonderful events of the night before, she sat up in bed and looked around. Drusilla was still asleep and snoring very loudly, but Sweetest Susan jumped out of bed and shook her by the shoulder.

"Drusilla! Drusilla! wake up!" cried Sweetest Susan. Drusilla stopped short in her snoring and turned over with a groan. She kept her eyes closed, and in a moment she would have been snoring again, but Sweetest Susan continued to shake her and called her until she squalled out: —

"Who dat? What you want? Oh, Lordy!"

"Wake up, Drusilla," said Sweetest Susan, "I want to ask you something."

"Ain't I 'wake? How kin I be any 'waker when I'm 'wake? Oh, is dat you, honey? I wuz skeer'd 't was dat lil' bit er ol' 'oman. Whar she gone? Las' time I seed her she wuz des walkin' 'roun' here like she wuz gwine ter tromple on me. I laid low, I did."

Sweetest Susan clasped her hands together and cried: "Oh, was n't it a dream, Drusilla? Did it all happen sure enough?"

Drusilla shook her head wildly. "How kin we bofe have de same kind er dream? I seed de 'oman gwine on, en you seed 'er gwine on. Uh-uh! Don't talk ter me 'bout no dreams."

The whole matter was settled when Buster John cried out from the next room: "What fuss was that you were making in there last night, squealing and squeaking?"

The matter was soon explained to Buster John, and after breakfast the children went out and sat on the big wood-pile and talked it all over. The boy asked a hundred questions, but still his curiosity was not satisfied.

All this time the birds were singing in the trees and the wood-sawyers sawing in the pine

logs. Jo-reeter, jo-reeter, jo-ree! sang the birds.
Craik, craik, craik, went the wood-sawyers.

"There are fifty dozen of them," said Buster
John.

"Fifty-five thousand you'd better say," replied
Sweetest Susan. "Just listen!"

"No needs ter listen," cried Drusilla. "You'd
hear 'em ef you plugged up yo' years."

Buster John put his knife-blade under a thick
piece of pine bark and pried it up to find one
of the busy sawyers. The bark was strong, but
presently it seemed to come up of its own accord,
and out jumped the queerest little man they had
ever seen or even heard of except in make-believe
story-books. Buster John dropped his knife,
and down it went into the wood-pile. He could
hear it go rattling from log to log nearly to the
bottom. Sweetest Susan gave a little screech.
Drusilla sat bolt upright and exclaimed: —

"You all better come en go see yo' ma. I
want ter see 'er myse'f."

But there was nothing to be frightened at. The
tiny man had brushed the dust and trash from
his clothes, and then turned to the children with
a good-humored smile. He was not above four

inches high. He had on a dress-coat. Drusilla afterward described it as a claw-hammer coat, velveteen knickerbockers, and silver buckles on his shoes. His hat was shaped like a thimble, and he had a tiny feather stuck in the side of it.

"I'm much obliged to you for getting me out of that scrape," he said with a bow to all the children. "It was a pretty tight place. I stayed out last night just one second and a half too late, and when I went to go home I found the door shut. So I just crawled under the bark there for a nap. The log must have turned in some way, for when I woke up and tried to crawl out I found I couldn't manage it. I wouldn't have minded that so much, but just then I saw one of those terrible flat-headed creatures making his way toward me. Why, his head was a sawmill! He was gnawing the wood out of his way and clearing a road to me. I tried to draw my sword, but I couldn't get it from under me. Then I felt the bark rising. I pushed as hard as I could, and here I am."

"Ax 'im his name," said Drusilla in an awe-stricken tone.

"Ah, I forgot," responded the little man. "I

know you, but you don't know me. My name is
Mr. Thimblefinger, and I shall be happy to serve
you. Whenever you want me just tap three
times on the head of your bed."

" Thank goodness! I don't sleep in no bed,"
exclaimed Drusilla.

" That makes no difference," said Mr. Thimblefinger. " If you sleep on a pallet just tap on the
floor."

" Please, Mister, don't talk dat a-way," pleaded
Drusilla, " kase I 'll be constant a-projeckin' wid
dat tappin', an' de fus' time you come I 'll holler
fire."

" Don't notice her," said Buster John, " she
talks to hear herself talk."

" I see," replied Mr. Thimblefinger, tapping
his forehead significantly and nodding his head.

" You kin nod," said Drusilla defiantly, " but
my head got mo' in it dan you kin comb out."

" I believe you!" exclaimed Mr. Thimblefinger, " I believe you!" He spoke so earnestly
that Sweetest Susan and Buster John laughed,
and Drusilla laughed with them.

" You dropped your knife," said Mr. Thimblefinger. " I 'm sorry of it. I can't bring it up

to you, but I'll see if I can't crawl under and get it out."

With that he leaped nimbly from log to log and disappeared under the wood-pile. The children went down to see what he would do. They were so astonished at his droll appearance that they forgot their curiosity.

"Is that a fairy, brother?" asked Sweetest Susan in a low voice.

"No!" exclaimed Buster John with a lofty air, but not loudly. "Don't you see he's not a bit like the fairies we read about in books? Why, he was afraid of a wood-sawyer."

"That's so," Sweetest Susan rejoined.

"He's a witch, dat what he is," said Drusilla.

"Shucks!" whispered Buster John. He heard the voice of Mr. Thimblefinger under the wood-pile.

"I've found it, I've found it!" he cried. And presently he made his appearance, dragging the knife after him. He tugged at it until he got it out, and then he sat down on a chip, wiped the perspiration from his eyes, and fanned himself with a thin flake of pine bark no bigger than a bee's wing.

"Pick me up and let's go on top of the wood-pile," said Mr. Thimblefinger after a while. "It's suffocating down here. Ouch! don't tickle me, if you do I shall have a fit." Buster John had lifted him by placing a thumb and forefinger under his arms. "And don't squeeze me, neither," the little man went on. "I was cramped under that bark until I'm as sore as a boil all over. Goodness! I wish I was at home!"

"Where do you live?" asked Sweetest Susan when they were once more seated on the wood-pile.

"Not far from here, not very far," replied Mr. Thimblefinger, shaking his head sagely, "but it is a different country — oh, entirely different."

Sweetest Susan edged away from the little man at this, and Drusilla stretched her eyes.

"What is it like?" asked Buster John boldly.

Mr. Thimblefinger reflected a while, and then shook his head. "I can show it to you," he said, "but I can't describe it."

"Pick 'im up an' show 'im to your ma!" exclaimed Drusilla suddenly.

"No, no, no!" cried Mr. Thimblefinger, leaping to his feet. "That would spoil everything.

No grown person living in this country has ever
seen me. No, no! don't try that. It would
spoil your luck. I would n't be here now if the
Dolls' Grandmother had n't begged me to come
with her last night. But I 'll come to see you,"
— he pointed at Drusilla. "I 'll come often."

"I des said dat fer ter see what you 'd say, "
protested Drusilla. " You wan' gwine ter take
'im, wuz you, honey?" This question was ad-
dressed to Buster John, who scorned to answer it.

"Grown people would n't understand me,"
Mr. Thimblefinger explained. "They know a
great deal too much to suit me."

"How do you get to your country?" inquired
Buster John, who was keen for an adventure.

"The nearest way is by the spring," replied
Mr. Thimblefinger. "That is the only way you
could go."

"Can I go too?" asked Sweetest Susan. "And
Drusilla?"

"Oh, of course," said Mr. Thimblefinger,
shrugging his shoulders. "One can go or all can
go."

"Do you go down the spring branch?" asked
Buster John.

" No, no," replied Mr. Thimblefinger. " Below
the spring and below the branch."

" Do you mean under the spring?" Sweetest
Susan inquired, with some hesitation.

" That's it," cried Mr. Thimblefinger. " Right
down through the spring and under it."

" Why, we'd drown," said Sweetest Susan.
" The spring is deep."

" Well, you'll ha' ter 'skuze me," exclaimed
Drusilla. " Dat water's too wet fer me."

Buster John waited for an explanation, but
none was forthcoming.

" We couldn't go through the spring, you
know," he said presently.

" How do you know?" asked Mr. Thimblefinger slyly. " Did you ever try it?"

He asked each of the children this, and the
reply was that none of them had ever tried it.

" I put my foot in it once," said Buster John,
" and the water was just like other spring water.
I know we can't go through it."

" Come now!" Mr. Thimblefinger suggested,
" don't say you know. Sometimes people live to
be very old and don't know the very things they
ought to know."

"But I know that," replied Buster John confidently.

"Very well, then," said Mr. Thimblefinger, pulling out a tiny watch, "did you ever feel of the water in the spring at precisely nine minutes and nine seconds after twelve o'clock?"

"N-o-o-o," replied Buster John, taken by surprise, "I don't think I ever did."

"Of course not!" cried Mr. Thimblefinger gayly. "You had no reason. Well, at nine minutes and nine seconds after twelve o'clock the water in the spring is not wet. It is as dry as the air we breathe. It is now two minutes after twelve o'clock. We'll go to the spring, wait until the time comes, and then you will see for yourselves."

As they went toward the spring — Mr. Thimblefinger running on before with wonderful agility — Drusilla touched Sweetest Susan on the arm. "Honey," said she, "don't let dat creetur pull you in de spring. Goodness knows, ef he puts his han' on me I'm gwine ter squall."

"Will you hush?" exclaimed Buster John impatiently.

"Watch out, now," said Drusilla defiantly.

"Ef you gits drownded in dar I'll sho' tell yo' ma."

Fortunately, there was no one near the spring, so Mr. Thimblefinger advanced boldly, followed closely by the children, though Drusilla seemed to hang back somewhat doubtfully. When they arrived there Mr. Thimblefinger took out his tiny timepiece and held it in his hand. The children watched him with breathless interest, especially Buster John, who was thrilled with the idea of having an adventure entirely different from any that he had read of in the story-books.

As the little man stood there holding his watch and looking at it intently, the dinner-bell rang, first in the hallway and then in the back porch. The children remembered it afterward.

"You all better go git yo' dinner 'fo' it git col', stidder projeckin' 'roun' here wid you dunner what," remarked Drusilla.

"Now!" exclaimed Mr. Thimblefinger, "put your hand in the spring."

Buster John did as he was bid, and, to his amazement, he could feel no water. He could see it, but he couldn't feel it. He turned pale with excitement and withdrew his hand. Then he put his other hand in, but the result was the same. He plunged his arm in up to the elbow, but his sleeve remained perfectly dry.

"Try it, sis," he cried.

Sweetest Susan did so, and boldly declared there was no water in the spring. She wanted Drusilla to try to wet her hand, but Drusilla sullenly declined.

Mr. Thimblefinger settled the matter by walking into the spring.

"Now, then, if you are going, come along," he cried. "You have just seventeen and a half seconds." He waved his hand from the bottom of the spring and stood waiting. A spring lizard ran near him, and he drew his sword and chased it into a hole. A crawfish showed its head, and he drove it away. Then he waved his hand again. "Come on, the coast is clear."

Buster John put his hand in the water again, and this seemed to satisfy him. He stepped boldly into the spring, and in a moment he stood by Mr. Thimblefinger, laughing, but still excited by the novelty of his experience. He called to his sister : —

"Come on, sis. It's splendid down here."

"Is it wet?" she asked plaintively. "Is it cold?"

"No!" replied Buster John impatiently. "Don't be a baby."

"Come on, Drusilla! You've got to come. Mamma said you must go wherever we went," cried Sweetest Susan.

"No, ma'am!" exclaimed Drusilla, with emphasis. "She ain't tol' me ter foller you in de fier an' needer in de water!"

But Sweetest Susan did n't wait to hear. She jumped into the spring with a splash and then stood by her brother very red in the face.

"Five more seconds!" cried Mr. Thimblefinger in a businesslike way.

Drusilla looked in the spring and hesitated. She could see the water plain enough, but then she could also see Sweetest Susan and Buster John, and they seemed to be very comfortable.

"I'm comin'," she yelled, "but ef you all make me git drownded in dry water I'll ha'nt you ef it's de las' thing I do!"

Then she shut her eyes tight, put her fingers in her ears, and leaped into the spring. She floundered around with her eyes still shut, and

gasped and caught her breath just like a drown-
ing person, until she heard the others laughing
at her, and then she opened her eyes with astonishment.

Suddenly there was a loud, splashing sound
heard above and around them and under their
feet.

"Watch out!" cried Mr. Thimblefinger.
"Run this way! The water is getting wet
again!"

The way seemed to widen before them as they
ran, and in a moment they found themselves
below the "gum," or "curb," of the spring and
beyond it. But as they went forward the bottom of the spring seemed to grow and expand,
and the sun shining through gave a soft light
that was very pleasant to the eye. The grass
was green and the leaves of the trees and the
flowers were pale pink and yellow.

Mr. Thimblefinger seemed to be very happy.
He ran along before the children as nimbly as a
killdee, talking and laughing all the time. Presently Drusilla, who brought up the rear, suddenly stopped in her tracks and looked around.
Then she uttered an exclamation of fright.

Sweetest Susan and Buster John paused to see what was the matter.

"Wharbouts did we come in at?" she asked.

Then, for the first time, the children saw that the bottom of the spring had seemed to expand, until it spread over their heads and around on all sides as the sky does in our country.

"Don't bother about that," said Mr. Thimblefinger. "No matter how big it looks, it's nothing but the bottom of the spring after all."

"But how are we to get out, please?" asked Sweetest Susan.

"The same way you came in," said Mr. Thimblefinger.

"I tol' you! I tol' you!" exclaimed Drusilla, swinging her right arm up and down vigorously. "Ef you kin fly you kin git out, an' you look much like flyin'. Dat what you git by not mindin' me an' yo' ma!"

"Tut! tut!" exclaimed Mr. Thimblefinger. "I'll 'sicc' the Katydids on you if you don't stop scaring the little girl. Come! we are not far from my house. We'll go there and see what the neighbors have sent in for dinner."

Buster John followed him as readily as before,

but Sweetest Susan and Drusilla were not so eager. They had no device, however, and Drusilla made the best of it.

"I ain't skeered ez I wuz. He talk mo' and mo' like folks."

So they went on toward Mr. Thimblefinger's house.

III.

"I HOPE you are not tired," said Mr. Thimblefinger to Sweetest Susan when they had been on their way for some little time. "Because if you are you can rest yourself by taking longer steps."

Buster John was ready to laugh at this, but he soon discovered that Mr. Thimblefinger was right. He found that he could hop and jump ever so far in this queer country, and the first use he made of the discovery was to jump over Drusilla's head. This he did with hardly any effort. After that the journey of the children, which had grown somewhat tiresome (though they would n't say so), became a frolic. They skimmed along over the gray fields with no trouble at all, but Drusilla found it hard to retain her balance when she jumped high. Mr. Thimblefinger, who had a reason for everything, was puzzled at this. He paused a while and stood thinking and rubbing his chin. Then he said that either Drusilla's head was too light or her heels too heavy — he couldn't for the life of him tell which.

There was one thing that bothered the children. If Mr. Thimblefinger's house was just big enough to fit him (as Buster John expressed it), how could they go inside? Sweetest Susan was so troubled that she asked Drusilla about it. But Drusilla shook her head vigorously.

"Don't come axin' me," she cried. "I done tol' you all right pine-blank not ter come. Ef de house lil' like dat creetur is, what you gwine do when night come? En den spozen 'pon top er dat dat a big rain come up? Oh, I tol' you 'fo' you started! Who in de name er sense ever heah talk er folks gwine down in a spring? You mought er know'd sump'in gwine ter happen. Oh, I tol' you!"

There was no denying this, and Sweetest Susan and her brother were beginning to feel anxious, when an exclamation from Mr. Thimblefinger attracted their attention.

"We are nearly there," he shouted. "Yonder is the house. My! won't the family be surprised when they see you!"

Sure enough there was the house, and it was not a small one, either. Drusilla said it looked more like a barn than a house, but Buster John said it did n't make any difference what it looked like so long as they could rest there and get something to eat, for they had had no dinner.

"I hope dey got sho 'nuff vittles — pot-licker an' dumplin's, an' sump'in you kin fill up wid," said Drusilla heartily.

Mr. Thimblefinger, who had been running a little way ahead, suddenly paused and waited for the children to come up.

"Come to think of it," he remarked, "you may have heard of some of my family. I call them my family, but they are no kin to me. We just live together in the same house for company's sake."

"They are not fairies?" suggested Sweetest Susan.

Mr. Thimblefinger shook his head. "Oh, no! Just common every-day people like myself. We put on no airs. Did you ever hear of Mrs. Meadows? And Mr. Rabbit? And Mrs. Rabbit?"

"Dem what wuz in de tale?" asked Drusilla.

"Yes," said Mr. Thimblefinger, "the very same persons."

"Sho 'nuff ! " exclaimed Drusilla. "Why, we been hear talk er dem sence 'fo' we wuz knee-high."

Sweetest Susan and Buster John said they had often heard of Mr. Rabbit and Mrs. Meadows. This seemed to please Mr. Thimblefinger very much. He smiled and nodded approval.

"Did they ever have you in a story ? " asked Buster John.

"No, no ! " replied Mr. Thimblefinger. "I was so little they forgot me." He laughed at his own joke, but it was very plain that he did n't relish the idea of not having his name in a book.

Presently the children came to the house, but they hesitated at the gate and stood there in fear and trembling. What they saw was enough to frighten them. An old woman was sitting in a chair knitting. She was not different from many old women the children had seen, but near her sat a Rabbit as big as a man. He was a tremendous creature, grizzly and gray, and watery-eyed from age. He sat in a rocking-chair smoking a pipe.

"Le' 's go back," whispered Drusilla. "Dat ar creetur bigger dan a hoss. Ef he git a glimp' us we er gone — gone!"

Sweetest Susan shivered and looked at Buster John, and Buster John looked at Mr. Thimblefinger. But Mr. Thimblefinger ran forward, crying out: —

"Howdy, folks, howdy! I've brought some friends home to dinner." He beckoned to the children. "Come on and see Mrs. Meadows and Mr. Rabbit."

Mrs. Meadows immediately dropped her knitting in her lap, and threw her hands up to her head, as if to arrange her hair.

"Come in," said Mr. Thimblefinger to the children.

"Yes, come on," exclaimed Mr. Rabbit in a voice that sounded as if he had a bad cold.

"I'm in no fix to be seen," said Mrs. Meadows, "but I'm glad to see you, anyhow. Come right in. Take off your things and make yourself at home. How did you get here? I reckon that little trick there has been telling tales out of school." She pointed at Mr. Thimblefinger and laughed.

"He brought us," said Sweetest Susan. "I'm sorry we came."

"Now, don't say that," remarked Mrs. Meadows kindly. "What are you afraid of?"

"Of him," replied Sweetest Susan, nodding her head toward Mr. Rabbit.

"Is that all?" exclaimed Mrs. Meadows. "Why, he's as harmless as a kitten."

"Yes, yes!" said Mr. Rabbit complacently. "No harm in me — no harm in old people. Just give us a little room in the corner — a little place where we can sit and nod — and there's no harm in us. I'm just as glad you've come as I can be. I see you've brought the Tar Baby. She's grown some since I saw her last." Mr. Rabbit looked at Drusilla with considerable curiosity. "I hope she's not as sticky as she used to be."

"Hey!" cried Buster John, laughing. "Mr. Rabbit thinks Drusilla is the Tar Baby!"

Drusilla tossed her head scornfully. "Huh! I ain't no Tar Baby. I may be a nigger, an' I speck I is, but I ain't no Tar Baby. My mammy done tol' me 'bout de Tar Baby in de tale, an' she got it fum her gran'daddy. Ef I'm

de Tar Baby, I 'm older dan my mammy's gran'-
daddy."

Mr. Rabbit took off his spectacles and wiped
them on his coat-tail. " My eyes are getting very
bad," he said, by way of apology. " But you
certainly look very much like the Tar Baby. If
you were both together in the dark, nobody
could tell you apart. Well, well! I 'm getting
old."

" You ain't no older dan you look," said Drusilla spitefully under her breath.

" Hush ! " whispered Sweetest Susan. " He 'll
eat us up."

Mrs. Meadows laughed. " Don't worry, child.
Mr. Rabbit loves his pipe and a joke, but he 'll
never hurt you. Never in the world."

" But this is n't in the world," suggested
Buster John.

" Well, it 's next door, as you may say," Mrs.
Meadows replied.

Just then Mr. Rabbit slowly raised himself
from his chair and examined the seat closely. " I
missed Mr. Thimblefinger," he said, " and I was
afraid I had sat on him."

" Oh, no ! " cried Mr. Thimblefinger, coming

out from under the steps; "I was just resting myself."

"Mr. Thimblefinger will take care of himself, I'll be bound," exclaimed Mrs. Meadows. "He's little; but is a mountain strong because it is big?"

"Why, that puts me in mind of the story — But never mind! I'm always thinking about old times." Mr. Rabbit sighed as he said this.

"Oh, please tell us the story," pleaded Sweetest Susan, anxious to make friends with Mr. Rabbit.

He shook his head. "Mrs. Meadows can tell it better than I can."

"Dinner!" cried Mr. Thimblefinger. "What about dinner?"

"Dinner'll be ready directly," replied Mrs. Meadows.

"But the story?" Sweetest Susan said.

THE STRONGEST — WHO? OR WHICH?

"Well," replied Mrs. Meadows, "it was like this: One time in the country where we came from — the country where you live now — there chanced to be a big frost, and the mill-pond froze over. Mr. Rabbit ran along that way and found that the pond had this bridge across it."

" Was it this Mr. Rabbit here ? " asked Buster John.

Mrs. Meadows folded her hands in her lap and looked at them. " Well," she said, " I never talk about folks behind their backs. You must do your own guessing. Anyway, Mr. Rabbit found the ice bridge over the pond, and as he was in something of a hurry he skipped across it. I mean he skipped a part of the way. The Ice was so slippery that when he got about halfway, his feet slipped from under him and he fell kerthump! He got up and rubbed himself as well as he could, and then he thought that the Ice must be very strong to hit him so hard a lick. He said to the Ice, ' You are very strong.'

" ' I am so,' replied the Ice.

" ' Well, if you are so strong, how can the Sun melt you ? '

" The Ice said nothing, and so Mr. Rabbit asked the Sun, ' Are you very strong ? '

" ' So they tell me,' replied the Sun.

" ' Then how can the Clouds hide you ? '

" The Sun was somewhat ashamed and had

nothing to say. So Mr. Rabbit looked at the Clouds.

" ' Are you very strong ? '

" ' We have heard so,' replied the Clouds.

" ' How can the Wind blow you ? '

" The Clouds sailed away, and Mr. Rabbit asked the Wind, ' Are you very strong ? '

" ' I believe you,' said the Wind.

" ' Then how can the Mountain stand against you ? '

" The Wind blew itself away, and then Mr. Rabbit asked the Mountain, ' Are you very strong ? '

" ' So it seems,' replied the Mountain.

" ' How can the Mouse make a nest in you ? '

" The Mountain was mum. So Mr. Rabbit asked the Mouse, ' Are you very strong ? '

" ' I believe so,' replied the Mouse.

" ' How can the Cat catch you ? '

" The Mouse hid in the grass. Mr. Rabbit asked the Cat, ' Are you very strong ? '

" ' Yes, indeed,' replied the Cat.

" ' How can the Dog chase you ? '

" The Cat began to wash her face. Then Mr. Rabbit said to the Dog, ' Are you very strong ? '

" ' I certainly am,' replied the Dog.

" ' Then why does the Stick scare you ? '

" The Dog began to scratch the fleas off his neck, and Mr. Rabbit said to the Stick, ' Are you very strong ? '

" ' Everybody says so.'

" ' Then how can the Fire burn you ? '

" The Stick was dumb, and Mr. Rabbit asked the Fire, ' Are you very strong ? '

" ' Anybody will tell you so,' the Fire answered.

" ' How can the Water quench you ? '

" The Fire hid behind the smoke. Then Mr. Rabbit asked the Water, ' Are you very strong ? '

" ' Strong is no name for it,' said the Water.

" ' How can the Ice cover you ? '

" The Water went running down the river, and after it had gone the Ice said to Mr. Rabbit, ' You see you had to come back to me at last.'

" ' Yes,' replied Mr. Rabbit, ' and now I am going away. You are too much for me.' Then Mr. Rabbit loped off, rubbing his bruises."

" Was it really you, Mr. Rabbit ? " asked Sweetest Susan.

Mr. Rabbit rubbed his mustache with the end

of his pipe-stem. "Well, I'll tell you the truth. I was mighty foolish in my young days. But now all I want to do is to eat breakfast, and then wait until dinner is ready, and then sit and wait until supper is put on the table."

Mrs. Meadows winked at the children and then turned to Mr. Rabbit.

"Now," said she, "I've told the story you ought to have told, for you know more about it than anybody else. It's as little as you can do to sing the old song that you sung when you used to go frolicking."

"Why, it's about myself!" exclaimed Mr. Rabbit. "At my time of life it would never do."

"Please make him sing it," said Sweetest Susan, who was much given to getting her own way by the pretty little art of coaxing.

"Oh, he'll sing it," replied Mrs. Meadows confidently. "He can't refuse."

Mr. Rabbit shook his head, and then seemed to fall into a brown study, but suddenly, seeing that they were all waiting for the song, he cleared up his throat, and after several false starts sang this song : —

OH, THIS IS MR. RABBIT!

Oh, this is Mr. Rabbit, that runs on the grass,
So rise up, ladies, and let him pass ;
He courted Miss Meadows, when her ma was away,
He crossed his legs, and said his say.
He crossed his legs, and he winked his eye,
And then he told Miss Meadows good-by.
    So it 's good-by, ducky,
      And it 's good-by, dear !
     I 'll never come to see you
      Until next year !
For this is Mr. Rabbit, that runs on the grass,
So rise up, ladies, and let him pass.

And he cried from the gate, so bold and free :
"I know you are glad to get rid of me."
And then Miss Meadows shook her head —
"If you stay too long you 'll find me dead.
    And it 's good-by, ducky,
      And it 's good-by, dear !
     You 'll find me dead
      When you come next year !"
For this is Mr. Rabbit, that runs on the grass,
So rise up, ladies, and let him pass.

Mr. Owl called out from the top of the tree,
"Oh, who ? Oh, who ?" and "He-he-he !"
Mr. Fox slipped off in the woods and cried ;
Mr. Coon's broken heart caused a pain in his side.
    For it 's good-by, ducky,
      And it 's good-by, dear !
     If you ever come to see me,
      Come before next year !

For this is Mr. Rabbit, that runs on the grass,
So rise up, ladies, and let him pass.

Mr. Rabbit looked around, and saw all the trouble,
And he laughed and he laughed till he bent over double.
He shook his head, and said his say —
" I 'll come a-calling when to-morrow is to-day.
   For when you have a ducky,
    Don't stay — don't stay —
   Go off and come again
    When to-morrow is to-day."
For this is Mr. Rabbit, that runs on the grass,
So rise up, ladies, and let him pass.

IV.

THERE is no doubt the children were very much surprised to see Mr. Rabbit. They were astonished to find that he was so large and solemn-looking. When the negroes on the plantation told them about Mr. Rabbit — or Brother Rabbit, as he was sometimes called — they had imagined that he was no larger than the rabbits they saw in the sedge-field or in the barley-patch, but this Mr. Rabbit was larger than a dozen of them put together.

In one way or another Sweetest Susan and Buster John and Drusilla showed their amazement very plainly — especially Drusilla, who took no pains to conceal hers. Every time Mr. Rabbit moved she would nudge Sweetest Susan or Buster John and exclaim: "Look at dat!" or, "We better be gwine!" or, "Spozen Brer Fox er Brer Wolf come up an' dey er dat big!"

Mrs. Meadows noticed this; indeed, she could not help noticing it. And so she said: —

"I reckon maybe you expected to find Mr. Rabbit no bigger than the rest of his family that live in your country."

Before the children could make any answer, Mr. Rabbit began to chuckle, and he chuckled so heartily that Sweetest Susan was afraid he would choke.

"I don't wonder you laugh," said Mrs. Meadows, elevating her voice a little, as if Mr. Rabbit were a little deaf.

"It may not be polite to laugh in company," replied Mr. Rabbit, "but I am obliged to do it." His voice was wheezy, and he nodded his head vigorously. "Yes, I am obliged to do it. Why, I could put one of those poor creatures in my coat-pocket. They are not Rabbits. They are Runts. Yes, Runts. That's what they are. And to think, too, that their great-grandparents might have come here when I did. But, no! They wouldn't hear to it. No new country for them, they said. And so they stayed where they were, and the breed has dwindled down to — to nothing. I'll be bound they have forgotten how to talk." He turned to the children with a look of inquiry.

" Why, of course, rabbits can't talk," said Buster John.

Mr. Rabbit shook his head sadly and put his hand to his eyes. " Well, well, well ! " he exclaimed after a while. " Can't talk ! But I might have known it. The family's gone to seed. I'm glad I'm not there to see it all. A neighbor here and there does no harm, but when people began to crowd in I concluded to move, and I'm glad I did. I'm old and getting feeble, but, thank gracious, I'm not a Runt."

" I don't see but you're as nimble as ever you were," remarked Mrs. Meadows soothingly.

" I know — I know ! " Mr. Rabbit insisted ; " I may be as nimble, but I'm not as keen for a frolic as I used to be. The chimney-corner suits me better than a barbecue." Mr. Rabbit closed his big eyes and sighed. " Well, well — everybody to his time, everybody to his taste ! "

Mrs. Meadows nodded her head approvingly. " Yes ; between first one thing and then another, there's lots of time and a heap of tastes."

" They tell me," remarked Mr. Rabbit suddenly, " that things have got to that pass in the country we came from that even Mr. Billy-Goat, who used to eat meat, has dwindled away in mind and body till he hangs around the stable doors and eats straw for a living. That's what Mr. Thimblefinger says, and he ought to know. I suppose Billy is still bob-tailed? I remember the very day he had his tail broken off."

"Tell us about it," remarked Buster John.

WHY MR. BILLY-GOAT'S TAIL IS SHORT.

"Oh, it does n't amount to much," said he. "It's hardly worth talking about. I think it was one Saturday. In those days, you know, we used to have a half-holiday every Saturday. We worked hard all the week, and we tried to crowd as much fun into a half-holiday as possible. Well, one Saturday afternoon Mr. Billy-Goat and Mr. Dog were walking arm in arm along the road, talking and laughing in a sociable way, when all of a sudden a big rain came up. Mr. Billy-Goat said he was mighty sorry he left his parasol at home, because the rain was apt to make his horns rust. Mr. Dog shook himself and said he did n't mind water, because when he got wet the fleas quit biting.

"But Mr. Billy-Goat hurried on and Mr. Dog kept up with him until they came to Mr. Wolf's house, and they ran into the front porch for shelter. The door was shut tight, but Mr. Billy-Goat had on his high-heel shoes that day, and he made so much noise as he tramped about that Mr. Wolf opened his window and looked out. When he saw who it was, he cried out : —

" 'Hallo! this is not a nice day to pay visits, but since you are here, you may as well come in out of the wet.'

"But Mr. Dog shook his head and flirted up dirt by scratching on the ground with his feet. He had smelled blood. Mr. Billy-Goat saw how Mr. Dog acted, and he was afraid to go in. So he shook his horns.

" 'You'd just as well come in and sit by the fire,' said Mr. Wolf, unlatching the door.

"But Mr. Dog and Mr. Billy-Goat thanked him kindly, and said they didn't want to carry mud into the house. They said they would just stand in the porch till the shower passed over. Then Mr. Wolf took down his fiddle, tuned it up, and began to play. In his day and time few could beat him playing the fiddle. And this time he played his level best, for he knew that if he could start Mr. Billy-Goat to dancing he'd have him for dinner."

"I don't see how," said Buster John.

"Well," exclaimed Mr. Rabbit, "if Mr. Billy-Goat began to dance he would be likely to dance until he got tired, and then it would be an easy matter for Mr. Wolf to outrun him."

"Of course," said Sweetest Susan.

"Well," Mr. Rabbit continued, "Mr. Wolf kept on playing the fiddle, but Mr. Billy-Goat did n't dance. Not only that, he kept so near the edge of the porch that the rain drifted in on his horns and ran down his long beard. But he kept his eye on Mr. Wolf. After playing the fiddle till he was tired, Mr. Wolf asked : —

" ' How do you get your meat, my young friends ? '

" Mr. Dog said he depended on his teeth, and Mr. Billy-Goat, thinking to be on the safe side, said he also depended upon his teeth.

" ' As for me,' cried Mr. Wolf, ' I depend on my feet ! ' and with that he dropped his fiddle and jumped at Mr. Billy-Goat. But he knocked the broom down and the handle tripped him. It

was all very sudden, but by the time Mr. Wolf
had recovered himself Mr. Billy-Goat and Mr.
Dog had gone a considerable distance.

"They ran and ran until they came to a big
creek. Mr. Billy-Goat asked Mr. Dog how he
was going to get across.

" 'Swim,' said Mr. Dog.

" 'Then I 'll have to bid you good-by,' replied
Mr. Billy-Goat, ' for I can't swim a stroke.'

"By this time they had arrived at the bank of
the creek, and they could hear Mr. Wolf coming
through the woods. They had no time to lose.
Mr. Dog looked around on the ground, gathered
some jan-weed, yan-weed, and tan-weed, rubbed
them together, and squeezed a drop of the juice
on Mr. Billy-Goat's horns. He had no sooner
done this than Mr. Billy-Goat was changed into
a white rock.

"Then Mr. Dog leaped into the creek and
swam across. Mr. Wolf ran to the bank, but
there he stopped. The water was so wide it
made tears come in his eyes; so deep that it made
his legs ache; and so cold that it made his body
shiver.

"When Mr. Dog arrived safely on the other

side he cried out, ' Aha! you are afraid! You 've
drowned poor Mr. Billy-Goat, but you are afraid
of me. I dare you to fling a rock at me!'

"This made Mr. Wolf so mad that he seized
the white rock and threw it at Mr. Dog with all
his might. It fell near Mr. Dog, and instantly
became Mr. Billy-Goat again. But in falling a
piece was broken off, and it happened to be Mr.
Billy-Goat's tail. Ever since then he has had a
very short tail."

"Were you there, Mr. Rabbit?" asked Sweetest Susan bluntly.

"I was fishing at the time," replied Mr. Rabbit. "I heard the noise they made, and I turned
around and saw it just as I 've told you."

Drusilla touched Buster John on the arm.
"We ain't dreamin', is we, honey?"

Buster John looked at her scornfully. "What
put that in your head?" he asked.

"Suppose the rock had hit Mr. Dog?" suggested Sweetest Susan.

THE PUMPKIN-EATER.

"Now, that 's so!" exclaimed Mr. Thimblefinger. "And it reminds me of a little accident

that happened in my mother's family. But it's
hardly worth telling."

" Well, tell it, anyhow," said Mrs. Meadows.

" Yes," remarked Mr. Rabbit, " the proof of
the pudding is in chewing the bag."

" Well," said Mr. Thimblefinger, "as far back
as I can remember, and before that, too, my
mother was a widow, and she had a great many
children to take care of. The reason she had so
many children was because she was poor. I have
noticed all my life that when people are very
poor they happen to have more children than
they know what to do with. This was the way
with my mother. She had a houseful of children, and she found it a hard matter to get
along.

" One day she went down to the creek to wash
the clothes, such as she and the children had, and
when she got there she found an old man sitting
on the bank. He said, ' Howdy,' and she said,
' Good-morning,' and then he asked her if she
would be so good as to wash his coat and his
waistcoat. She said she would be glad to do
so, and the old man said he would be very much
obliged. So my mother washed the coat and

waistcoat. Then he asked her if she would comb his hair for him, and she did so.

"The old man thanked her kindly, and took from his pocket a string of red beads and made her a present of them. Then he told her to go out behind the house when she got home, and there she'd find a pumpkin-tree growing. He said that she must bury the string of beads at the foot of the tree.

"'That's a pity,' exclaimed my mother; 'they are so beautiful.'

"But the old man declared that she must do as he said, and after that she was to go to the pumpkin-tree every day and ask for as many pumpkins as she wanted.

"My mother went home and found the pumpkin-tree where never a tree had been growing before, and at its roots she buried the string of beads. Next morning, bright and early, she went to the pumpkin-tree and called for one pumpkin. Down it dropped from the tree. For a long time my mother and her children were happy and growing fat. Every day a big pumpkin would be cooked, and as my mother had to leave us so as to attend to her work, enough

pumpkin would be left in the pot to last us all day.

"I remember that time very well," Mr. Thimblefinger continued, with a sigh, "for I was getting fat and growing to be almost as large as the rest of the children. But one day, as my mother was going out to work she found a hamper basket on the gate-post, and in that basket was a baby. So she carried the baby in the house, gave it something to eat, and then put it on the floor to play with the rest. But as soon as she got out of the yard the baby crawled to the pot where the cooked pumpkin was, and ate and ate until there was no pumpkin left. Of course, the rest of the children had to go hungry. And when my mother came home she had to go hungry, too.

"She was very much surprised. She found all the pumpkin gone and the children crying for something to eat, and the stray baby was crying louder than any. She said we were the greediest children she had ever seen.

"The next day she cooked two pumpkins, but the same thing happened. The baby went to the pot and ate both. The children told her how it happened, but she wouldn't believe them. She said she couldn't be made to believe that one puny little baby could eat two whole pumpkins — and it *is* very queer, when you come to think about it.

"The next day she cooked three pumpkins, but the same thing happened. Then four, then five, then six. But it was always the same. No matter how many pumpkins were cooked, the stray baby would eat them all, and the rest of the children would have to go hungry. You see how small I am," said Mr. Thimblefinger, suddenly pausing in the thread of his story. "Well, the reason of it is that I was starved out by that pumpkin-eating baby. My brothers and sisters and myself were just as large and as healthy as any other children until that baby was found on the gate-post, and from that day we began to dwindle and shrink away.

"Well, we starved and starved until at last my mother could very plainly see that something was the matter. So she set a trap for the baby and baited it with pumpkins. She hadn't got out of hearing before the baby put his head in the pot and got caught in the trap. It stayed there all

day, and when mother came home at night she
found it there. She was very much surprised,
but she saw she must get rid of the baby. She
said that any creature that could manage to eat
like that was able to take care of itself, and so
she carried it off down the road and left it
there.

"Now this Pumpkin-Eater was a witch baby,
and as soon as it thought my mother was out of
sight and hearing it changed itself into a tall,
heavy man."

"'T wuz feedin' de big man all de time," exclaimed Drusilla.

"Certainly," replied Mr. Thimblefinger. "My
mother was watching it, and she followed to see
where it would go. It went down to the bank of
the river. There it found the old man who had
given my mother the string of beads, and asked
him for something to eat.

"'Comb my hair for me,' said the old man.

"But it refused, and then the old man told it
to go to the pumpkin-tree and ask for twenty
pumpkins. The greedy thing was glad to do this.
It went to the tree and called for twenty pumpkins, and down they fell on its head."

"What then?" asked Buster John, as Mr. Thimblefinger paused.   "Was it hurt?"

"Smashed!"   exclaimed Mr. Thimblefinger. "Knocked flatter than a pancake! Broke into jiblets!"

"It was a great waste of pumpkins," remarked Mrs. Meadows.

V.

THE TALKING-SADDLE.

JUST then Mrs. Meadows smoothed out her apron and rose from her chair.

"I smell dinner," she said, "and it smells like it is on the table. Let's go in and get rid of it."

She led the way, and the children followed. The dinner was nothing extra, — just a plain, every-day, country dinner, with plenty of pot-liquor and dumplings; but the children were hungry, and they made short work of all that was placed before them. Drusilla waited on the table, as she did at home, but she didn't go close to Mr. Rabbit. She held out the dishes at arm's length when she offered him anything, and once she came very near dropping a plate when he suddenly flapped his big ear on his nose to drive off a fly.

Mrs. Meadows was very kind to the children, but when once the edge was taken off their appetite they began to get uneasy again. There were a thousand questions they might have asked, but they had been told never to ask questions in company. Mr. Thimblefinger, who had a keen eye for such things, noticed that they were beginning to get glum and dissatisfied, and so he said with a laugh : —

"I've often heard in my travels of children who talked too much, but these don't talk at all."

"Oh, they'll soon get over that," Mrs. Meadows remarked. "Everything is so strange here, they don't know what to make of it. When I was a little bit of a thing my ma used to take me to quiltings, and I know it took me the longest kind of a time to get used to the strangers and all."

"This isn't a quilting," said Sweetest Susan, with a sigh ; "I wish it was."

"I don't!" exclaimed Buster John plumply.

"Once when I was listening through a key-hole," said Mr. Thimblefinger, placing his tiny knife and fork crosswise on his plate, "I heard a story about a Talking-Saddle."

"Tell it! tell it!" cried Buster John and Sweetest Susan.

"I suppose you have no pie to-day?" said Mr. Rabbit.

"Oh, yes," said Mrs. Meadows, "we'll have the pie and the story, too."

Mr. Thimblefinger smacked his lips and winked his eye in such comical fashion that the children laughed heartily, but they didn't forget the story.

"I don't know that I can remember the best of it," said Mr. Thimblefinger. "The wind was blowing and the keyhole was trying to learn how to whistle, and I may have missed some of the story. But it was such a queer one, and I was listening so closely, that I came very near falling off the door-knob when some one started to come out. I think we'd better eat our pie first. I might get one of those huckleberries in my throat while talking, and there's no doctor close at hand to keep me from choking to death."

So they ate their huckleberry-pie, and then Mr. Thimblefinger told the story.

"Once upon a time a farmer had five sons. He was not rich and he was not poor. He had some land, and he had a little money. He divided his land equally among his four oldest sons, giving each just as much as he could till. To each, he also gave a piece of money. Then he called his youngest son, and said : —

" ' You have sharp eyes and a keen wit. You want no land. All you need is a saddle. That I will give you.'

" ' A saddle! What will I do with a saddle ? ' asked the youngest son, whose name was Tip-Top.

" ' Make your fortune with it.'

" ' If I had a horse — '

" ' A head is better than a horse,' the father replied.

" Not long after, the old man died. The land was divided up among the four older sons, and Tip-Top was left with the saddle. He slung it on his back and set out to make his fortune. It was not long before he came to a large town. He rested for a while and then he went into the town. He remembered that his father had said a head was better than a horse, so, instead of carrying the saddle on his back, he put it on his head. At first the people thought he was carrying the saddle because he had sold his horse for a good price, or because the animal had died. But he went through street after street still carrying the saddle on his head, never pausing to look around or to speak to anybody, and at last the people began to wonder. Some said he was a simpleton, some said he was a saddle-maker advertising his wares, and some said he was a tramp who ought to be arrested and put in the workhouse.

"This talk finally reached the ears of the Mayor of the town, and he sent for Tip-Top to appear before him."

"What is a Mayor?" asked Sweetest Susan suddenly.

"He de head patter-roller," said Drusilla, before anybody else could reply.

"That's about right," Mr. Thimblefinger declared. "Well, the Mayor sent for Tip-Top. But instead of going to the place where the Mayor held his court, Tip-Top inquired where his house was and went there. Now, when Tip-Top knocked at the Mayor's door the servant, seeing the man with a saddle on his head, began to scold him.

"'Do you think the Mayor keeps his harness in the parlor? Go in the side gate and carry the saddle in the cellar where it belongs. Hang it on the first peg you see.'

"Tip-Top tried to say something, but the servant shut the door with a bang. Then Tip-Top

did as he was bid. He went through the side
gate, and found the cellar without any trouble,
but instead of hanging the saddle on a peg, he
placed it on the floor and sat on it.

"After waiting patiently a while, wondering
when the Mayor would call him, Tip-Top heard
voices on the other side of the wall. He listened
closely, and soon found that the housemaid who
had driven him away from the Mayor's door was
talking to her brother, who had just returned
from a long journey.

"'The Mayor has gold,' said the brother.
'You must tell me where he keeps it. I have a
companion in my travels, and to-night we shall
come and take the treasure.'

"For a long time the housemaid refused to
tell where the Mayor kept his gold, but the brother threatened and coaxed, and finally she told
him where the treasure lay.

"'It is in a closet by the chimney in the first
room to the right at the head of the stairs. The
gold is in an iron box and it is very heavy.'

"'My companion has long hair and a strong
arm,' said the brother. 'He is cross-eyed and
knock-kneed. It wouldn't do for you to meet

him in the hallway. Go to bed early and lock your door, and if you hear any outcry during the night cover your head with a pillow and go to sleep again.'

"Then the housemaid and her brother went away.

"'Well,' said Tip-Top, 'this is no place for me.'

"He waited a while, and then went out of the cellar into the yard with his saddle on his head. The cook, seeing him there, told him to carry the saddle to the stable where the horses were kept. Tip-Top went to the stable, placed his saddle in an empty stall, and sat on it.

"After a while he heard two persons come in from the street. They went into a stall near by and began to talk. One was the coachman and the other was his nephew, who had just returned from a long journey.

"'The Mayor has fine horses,' said the nephew. 'I must have two of them to-night, otherwise I am ruined forever.'

"The coachman refused to listen at first, but after a while he consented. He told his nephew that the stable-boy slept in the manger.

" ' I have a companion in my travels,' said his nephew, ' and to-night we shall come and take the horses away. My companion has short hair and a heavy hand. Close your eyes and cover your head with straw if you hear any outcry.'

" After a while the coachman and his nephew went out into the street again, and then Tip-Top came forth from the stable with the saddle on his head. The Mayor had just come in, and was standing at his window. He saw the man in the yard with the saddle on his head, and sent a servant to call him.

" ' What is your name ? ' asked the Mayor.

" ' Tip-Top, your honor.'

" ' I did n't ask after your health ; I asked for your name,' said the Mayor.

" ' It is Tip-Top, your honor.'

" ' Your name or your health ? '

" ' Both, your honor.'

" ' What are you doing here ? '

" ' His honor, the Mayor, sent for me, your honor.'

" ' What were you doing just now ? '

" ' Waiting to be sent for, your honor.'

" ' Where is your horse ? ' asked the Mayor.

" ' I have no horse, your honor.'

" ' Why do you carry your saddle?'

" ' Because no one will carry it for me, your honor.'

" ' Why do you not sell it and be rid of it, ninny?'

" ' Few are rich enough to buy it, your honor.'

" ' How much money is it worth?'

" ' Two thousand pieces of gold, your honor.'

" ' Are you crazy?' cried the Mayor. ' Why is it so valuable?'

" ' It is a Talking-Saddle, your honor.'

" ' What does it say?'

" ' Everything, your honor. It warns, it predicts, and it gives advice.'

" ' Let it talk for me,' said the Mayor, full of curiosity.

" ' Your honor would fail to understand its language,' replied Tip-Top.

" ' Let it talk and do you tell me what it says.'

" Tip-Top placed his saddle on the carpet and pressed his foot against it until the leather made a creaking noise.

" ' I am waiting,' said the Mayor. ' What does the saddle say?'

" ' It says, your honor, that you must call the housemaid.'

" The Mayor, to humor the joke, did so. The housemaid came, grumbling. She looked at the saddle, at Tip-Top, and then at the Mayor.

" ' Now what does the saddle say ? ' asked the Mayor.

" ' It says, your honor, that this woman has a brother, who has just returned from a journey in strange lands. The saddle says, your honor, that this woman's brother has a companion who has long hair and a strong arm.'

" ' Is that all ? ' asked the Mayor.

" ' No, your honor, it is not half.'

" ' It is very strange,' said the housemaid.

" ' The saddle says, your honor, that if you will sit in the closet by the chimney, in the first room to the right, where there is an iron box that is very heavy, you will receive a visit to-night from this woman's brother and his companion.'

" The Mayor was very much astonished, but before he could open his lips the woman fell on her knees and confessed all. The Mayor called an officer and sent her away. Then he turned to Tip-Top, and asked : —

" ' Is that all ? '

" ' By no means, your honor. The saddle says send for the coachman.'

" The Mayor did so, and the coachman came, bowing and smiling.

" ' How much is the saddle worth ? ' the Mayor asked him.

" ' Master, it is worthless,' replied the coachman, with a sneer.

" ' Let us see,' said the Mayor. Then, turning to Tip-Top : ' What does the saddle say ? '

" ' It says, your honor, that this coachman here has a nephew, who has just returned from a long journey. It says that the nephew has a companion who has short hair and a heavy hand.'

" ' What more ? '

" ' The saddle says, your honor, that if you will sleep in the manger where your two finest horses feed, you will receive a visit from the coachman's nephew and his traveling companion.'

" The coachman implored his master's mercy, and told all. Of course, the Mayor was very much astonished. He turned his unfaithful servants over to an officer, and that night had a watch set around his house and stable, and caught the thieves and their companions."

"But the saddle did n't talk," said Sweetest Susan. "So the man did n't tell what was true." She made this remark with so much dignity that Mrs. Meadows laughed.

But Buster John was quite impatient.

"This is n't a girl's story," he exclaimed.

"Oh, yes," replied Mrs. Meadows. "It is for girls as well as boys. Sometimes people tell stories just to pass the time away, and if the stories have little fibs in 'em, that don't do anybody any harm, they just keep them in there. If they did n't, the story would n't be true."

"Is that the end of the story of the Talking-Saddle?" asked Buster John.

"No! Oh, no!" Mr. Thimblefinger answered. "I was just going to tell you the rest."

But before he could go on with it, the noise of laughter was heard at the door, and then there came running in a queer-looking girl and a very queer-looking boy.

VI.

THE queer-looking girl was running from the very queer-looking boy, and both were laughing loudly. When they saw the children sitting at the table they both stopped suddenly. The queer-looking girl turned and made a wry face at the very queer-looking boy. At this both burst out laughing, and suddenly stopped again.

"Be ashamed of yourselves!" exclaimed old Mr. Rabbit, rapping on the floor with his cane. "Be ashamed! Where are your manners? Go and speak to our friends and make your best bow, too, — don't forget that!" Mr. Rabbit appeared to be very indignant.

Mrs. Meadows was in a better humor. "This," she said, as the queer-looking girl came forward, "is Chickamy Crany Crow, and this, as the very queer-looking boy came timidly up, is Tickle-My-Toes."

They bowed, and then went off a little way,

looking very solemn and comical. They did n't dare glance at each other for fear they would begin laughing again. The reason they looked so queer was because, although they acted like children, they were old in appearance, — as old as a person past middle age.

"They are country-raised, poor things! You 'll have to excuse them. They don't know any better." Mr. Thimblefinger sighed as he said this, and looked thoughtful.

"What about the Talking-Saddle?" Buster John inquired. "You said the story was n't finished."

"To be sure! To be sure!" Mr. Thimblefinger cried. "My mind is like a wagon without a tongue. It goes every way but the right way. Where was I? Oh, yes, I remember now."

"Well, the Mayor was very thankful to Tip-Top for saving his treasure and his horses, but he was n't satisfied about the saddle. He was worried. Now, you know when a child is worried it cries, but when a grown man is worried he sits down and looks away off, and puts his elbow in his hand and his finger to his nose — so."

"Oh, I 've seen papa do that," laughed Sweetest Susan.

"Yes, that's the way the Mayor did," Mr. Thimblefinger continued. "There was a great thief in that country who had never been caught. He didn't care for judges and juries and court-houses. He always sent the Mayor word when he was coming to the city and when he was go-ing away.

"Now, the Mayor had received a letter from this man just the day before Tip-Top came. The thief said he was coming after a fine race-horse that was owned by the Mayor's brother. So the Mayor sat and thought, and finally he asked Tip-Top if his Talking-Saddle could catch a famous thief.

"'It has just caught four common rogues, your honor,' replied Tip-Top, 'and I think it can catch one uncommon thief.'

"Then the Mayor told Tip-Top that the most famous thief in all that country intended to steal his brother's race-horse. Tip-Top said he must see the horse, and together they went to the sta-ble where it was kept. The horse was already guarded. Two servants sat in the stall. two sat outside, and two remained near the door. The Mayor's brother was also there.

"'What is this?' the brother asked.

"'This fellow wants to sell his saddle,' replied the Mayor.

"'Then arrest him,' cried the brother, 'for he is the thief.'

"'Nonsense,' replied the Mayor. 'He is a very honest man and I will vouch for him.'

Then the Mayor called his brother aside and told him why the man with the saddle had come to see the horse.

"Tip-Top talked with the men who had been set to guard the horse, and he soon found that one of them was an accomplice of the thief. This man made a swift sign to Tip-Top, and placed his finger on his mouth. Tip-Top replied by closing his eyes with his fingers, as if to show that he saw nothing. When he had an opportunity he said to this man : —

"'Tell your master I will be willing to sell the saddle to-night. I will sleep with it under my head on the next corner. It is worth one thousand pieces of gold.'

"Then he returned to the Mayor, and they went away. Tip-Top laughed as they walked along. 'This thief,' he remarked, 'is a fool.

It is so easy to steal a horse that he will not buy a saddle. He will try to steal mine. Then we shall catch him. He will get the horse — '

" ' What ! ' cried the Mayor ; ' get the horse ? '

" ' Certainly ; nothing is easier,' replied Tip-Top. ' He will get the horse, and then he will want a saddle. He will be passing the wall here. He will see me sleeping with my head on my friend and then he will attempt to steal it, but the surcingle will be buckled around my body, and I will awake and cry blue murder. Then you and your brother can come forward from the vacant house yonder and seize him.'

" ' Where did you learn all this ? ' asked the Mayor. He began to suspect that his brother was right when he said that Tip-Top was the thief.

" ' My saddle told me,' Tip-Top answered.

" ' Well,' said the Mayor, ' your plan is as good as any, but how will the thief get the horse that is so well guarded ? '

" ' Ah ! ' Tip-Top exclaimed, ' if I were to tell you, we should never catch the thief.'

" So it was all arranged. Tip-Top was to sleep on his Talking-Saddle, near the wall and the

Mayor and his brother were to watch from the windows of the vacant house opposite.

"When night came, the watchers who had been set to guard the horse were very anxious. They were ready to arrest any one who might chance to enter. Whenever they heard footsteps approaching they seized their clubs and stood on the defensive. Sometimes a passer-by would pause, look in, and ask what the trouble was. Then the watchers would reply that they were waiting for the great thief who was coming to steal the fine horse. Thus the hours passed, but no thief came. Then the watchers began to get tired.

"'We are crazy,' said one. 'How can a thief steal this horse, even if he were to come in here? We are four to one. Two of us should sleep a while, and thus we can take turns in watching.' This was agreed to, and two of the guards stretched themselves on the straw and prepared to sleep. But just then they heard some one singing far down the street. It was a jolly song, and the sound of it came louder and louder. As the singer was going by, the light in the stable caught his eye, and he paused and looked in, but still kept up his singing.

" 'Friends,' he said when his song was done, 'what is the trouble?'

" 'We are watching a horse.'

" 'Is he sick? Perhaps I can aid you. I have doctored many a horse in my day.'

" 'He is not sick,' replied the watchers. 'He is well and taking his ease. We are watching to prevent a thief from stealing him.'

" Then they told him the threat the thief had made.

" 'Come, that is too good,' cried the newcomer. 'This thief will be worth looking at when four such stout lads as you get through with him. When does he show himself?'

" 'That is what we are to find out,' replied the watchers.

" 'Very well,' the newcomer said; 'I'll stay, by your permission, and see you double him up.'

" The watchers gave their consent gladly, for the newcomer had a lively manner and a rattling tongue. He sang songs and told stories for an hour or more, and then pulled a bottle from under his coat.

" 'A little wine,' he said, 'will clear the fog from our throats.' He passed the bottle around, and all drank except the guard who was watching in the stall.

"Now the man who had come singing up the street was the thief himself, and the guard in the stall was his companion. The wine was drugged, and in a very few minutes three of the watchers were fast asleep. Then the thief and his companion took the horse from the stall.

"'I shall have to remain here and pretend to be asleep,' said the companion. 'You will find a saddle around the corner.' He then told the thief about the man with the saddle.

"'You are a fool, my friend,' said the thief. 'It is a trick — a trap.'

"But when he had carried off the horse and hid it at the house of an acquaintance, the thought of the man with the saddle worried him so that he went back to satisfy himself. Tip-Top and his saddle were there, and Tip-Top had slept so soundly that his head had rolled from his pillow. The thief thought it would be a good stroke of business to take the saddle along, but when he tried to lift it, Tip-Top awoke and seized him, and cried 'Murder!' at the top of his voice.

"The Mayor and his brother rushed from

their place of concealment, and soon the thief was bound.

" ' Where is the horse ? ' cried the Mayor.

" ' What horse ?' exclaimed the thief. ' Do you think I carry horses in my pocket ? '

" ' What were you doing here, then ? '

" ' This fellow's head had slipped from its pillow, and when I tried to put it back he seized me and yelled that I was murdering him ! I saw no horse under the saddle.'

" ' Wait here a little,' said Tip-Top. ' Hold this thief till I return.'

" He went to the stable, woke the thief's accomplice, who by this time was really asleep, and told him his companion had been captured. ' If I can find the horse and hide it our friend will be safe, for nothing can be proved on him.'

" The man was so frightened that he told Tip-Top where he had arranged to meet the thief the next day. Then Tip-Top returned to the Mayor and his brother, who still held the thief, and took them to the house where the horse had been stabled.

" When the horse had been found and restored to its owner the Mayor said to Tip-Top that he would not only reward him handsomely but grant any request he might make.

"'Then, your honor,' replied Tip-Top, 'give this man his liberty.'

"'Why?' asked the Mayor, much astonished.

"'Because, your honor, he is my brother.'

"The thief was as much astonished as the Mayor at this turn in his affairs, but he had no difficulty in recognizing Tip-Top as his younger brother.

"'He certainly is a man of talent,' said the Mayor, 'and it is a pity that he should be executed.'

"Then the thief fell on his knees and begged the Mayor to pardon him, promising him to live and die an honest man. And he kept his promise. He engaged in business, and, aided by Tip-Top's advice and influence, made a large fortune."

"What became of the Talking-Saddle?" asked Buster John.

"Well," replied Mr. Thimblefinger, "Tip-Top hung the saddle in his front porch, as you have seen farmers do. He thought a great deal of it."

"I 've read something about the great thief," remarked Buster John. "But the story did n't end that way. The thief escaped every time."

"Oh, well, you know how some people are," exclaimed Mrs. Meadows. "They want everything to happen just so; even a thief must be a big man if he 's in a story; but I don't believe anybody ever stole anything yet without getting into trouble about it."

"Who is that crying?" Mr. Rabbit suddenly exclaimed.

"I hear no crying," said Mrs. Meadows.

"I certainly thought I heard crying," persisted Mr. Rabbit.

"It is Chickamy Crany Crow and Tickle-My-Toes singing. Listen!"

Sure enough the queer-looking boy and the queer-looking girl were singing a song. One sang one line and the other the next line, and this made the song somewhat comical. The words were something like these: —

CHICKAMY CRANY CROW.

Oh sing it slow,
This song of woe,
Of the girl who went to wash her toe!

Her name was Chick —
(Oh run here quick) —
The word 's so thick) —
Chickamy — Chickamy Crany Crow !

Chickamy what ? and Chickamy which ?
She went to the well and fell in the ditch ;
What o'clock, old Witch ?

The clock struck one
And bowed to the sun ;
But the sun was fast asleep you know ;
And the moon was quick,
With her oldtime trick —
To hide from Chick —
Chickamy — Chickamy Crany Crow !

Chickamy what ? and Chickamy which ?
She went to the well and fell in the ditch ;
What o'clock, old Witch ?

Oh, sad to tell !
She went to the well —
The time was as close to eve as to dawn —
To Chickamy Chick,
So supple and slick,
The clock said " Tick ! "
But when she came back her chicken was gone !

Oh, whatamy, whichamy, chickamy, oh !
Moonery, oonery, tickamy Toe !
Wellery, tellery, gittery go !
Witchery, itchery, knitchery know."

"What kinder gwines on is dat?" exclaimed Drusilla, whose mind had never been quite easy since she walked through the dry water in the spring without getting drowned. "We all better be makin' our way to'rds home. Time we git dar — ef we ever is ter git dar — it 'll be dark good. Den what yo' ma gwine to say? She gwine ter talk wid de flat er her han' — dat what she gwine ter talk wid. Come on!"

"Can't you be quiet?" cried Buster John. "It 's nothing but a song."

"Oh, you kin stay, an' I 'll stay wid you," said Drusilla; "but when Mistiss git you in de wash-room, don't you come sayin' dat I would n't fetch you home."

"I want to see everything," said Buster John.

"I done seed much ez I want ter see," replied Drusilla, "an' now I want ter live ter tell it."

Before Buster John could say anything more, everything suddenly grew a little darker, and in the middle of the sky — or what ought to have been the sky, but which was the enlarged bottom of the spring — there was a huge shadow. The children looked at it in silence.

VII.

THE LADDER OF LIONS.

THE shadow that seemed to fall over everything caused Buster John and Sweetest Susan and Drusilla to run to the door. It was not a very dark shadow, but it was dark enough to attract their attention and excite their alarm. They were not yet used to their surroundings, for, although a great many things they saw and heard were familiar to them, they could not forget that they had come through the water in the spring. They could not forget that Mr. Thimblefinger was the smallest grown person they had ever seen, — even if he were a grown person, — nor could they forget that they had never seen a rabbit so wonderfully large as Mr. Rabbit. Drusilla expressed the feelings of all when she remarked that she felt "skittish." They were ready to take alarm at anything that might happen. Therefore they ran to the door to see what the shadow meant. Finally they looked up at the sky, or what seemed to be

the sky, and there they saw, covering a large part
of it, the vague outline of a huge jug. The
shadow wobbled about and wavered, and ripples
of light and shadow played about it and ran
down to the horizon on all sides.

An astronomer, seeing these fantastic wobblings
and waverings of light and shadow in our firma-
ment, would straightway send a letter or a cable
dispatch to the newspapers, declaring that an un-
heard-of convulsion was shaking the depths of
celestial space. And, indeed, it was all very puz-
zling, even to the children, but Drusilla, who had
less imagination than any of the rest, accounted
for it all by one bold stroke of common sense.

"Shuh! 'T ain't nothin' 't all!" she exclaimed.
" Dey done got froo wid dinner at home, an' ol'
Aunt 'Cindy done put de buttermilk-jug back in
de spring."

Sweetest Susan caught her breath with a gasp,
and laughed hysterically. She had been very
much alarmed.

" I expect that's what it is," said Buster John,
but there was some doubt in his tone. He turned
to Mr. Thimblefinger, who had followed them.
" What time is it, please?"

Mr. Thimblefinger drew his watch from his pocket with as much dignity as he could assume, and held his head gravely on one side. "It is now — let me see — *ahem!* — it is now precisely thirteen minutes and eleven seconds after one o'clock."

"Is that the jug in the spring?" asked Sweetest Susan, pointing to the huge black shadow that was now wobbling and wavering more slowly.

Mr. Thimblefinger shaded his eyes with his hand and examined the shadow critically. "Yes, that is the jug — the light hurts my eyes — yes, certainly, that is the jug."

Presently a volume of white vapor shot out from the shadow. It was larger than the largest comet, and almost as brilliant.

"What is that?" asked Sweetest Susan.

Mr. Thimblefinger felt almost as thoughtful as a sure-enough man of science.

"That," said he, "is an emanation — an exhalation, you might say — that we frequently witness in our atmosphere."

"A which?" asked Buster John.

"Well," replied Mr. Thimblefinger, clearing his throat, "it's — er — an emanation."

"Huh!" cried Drusilla, "'t ain't no kind er nation. It's des de milk leakin' out'n dat jug. I done tol' Aunt 'Cindy 'bout dat leakin' jug."

Mr. Rabbit and Mrs. Meadows had come out of the house in time to hear this, and they laughed heartily. In fact, they all laughed except Mr. Thimblefinger and Drusilla.

"It happens every day," said Mrs. Meadows. "We never notice it. I suppose if it happened up there where you children live, everybody would make a great to-do? I'm glad I don't live there where there's so much fussing and guessing going on. I know how it is. Something happens that does n't happen every day, and then somebody 'll guess one way and somebody another way, and the first thing you know there 's a great rumpus over nothing. I'm truly glad I came away from there in time to get out of the worst of it. You children had better take a notion and stay here with us."

"Oh, no," cried Sweetest Susan. "Mamma and papa would want to see us."

"That 's so," said Mrs. Meadows. "Well, I just came out here to tell you not to get too near the Green Moss Swamp beyond the hill yonder.

There's an old Spring Lizard over there that might want to shake hands with you with his tail. Besides it's not healthy around there; it is too damp."

" Oh, we are not going anywhere until we start home," Sweetest Susan remarked.

" How large is the Spring Lizard?" inquired Buster John.

" He's a heap too big for you to manage," replied Mrs. Meadows. " I don't know that he'd hurt you, but he's slept in the mud over there until he's so fat he can't wallow scarcely. He might roll over on you and hurt you some."

" Are there any lions over there?" inquired Sweetest Susan.

" No, honey, not a living one," said Mrs. Meadows.

By this time Mr. Rabbit had come out on the piazza, bringing his walking-cane and his pipe. He presently seated himself on the steps, and leaned his head comfortably against one of the posts.

" Well, well, well," he exclaimed. " It has been years and years since I've heard the name of Brother Lion. Is he still living and doing well?"

Mr. Rabbit turned an inquiring eye on Sweetest Susan.

"She does n't know anything about lions," said Buster John.

" Why, I do ! " cried Sweetest Susan. " I saw one once in a cage."

" In a cage? Brother Lion in a cage ? " Mr. Rabbit raised his hands and rolled his eyes in astonishment. " What is the world coming to ? Well, I 've said many and many a time that Brother Lion was not right up here." Mr. Rabbit tapped his forehead significantly. " In a cage ! Now, that pesters me. Why, he used to go roaring and romping about the country, scaring them that did n't know him mighty nigh to death. And so Brother Lion is in a cage ? But I might have known it. I wonder how the rest of the family are getting on ? Not that they are any kin to me, for they are not. I called him Brother Lion just to be neighborly. Oh, no ! He and his family are no kin to me. They are too heavy in both head and feet for that."

Mr. Rabbit closed his eyes as if reflecting, and patted the ground softly with his foot.

" Well, well ! I remember just as well as if it

were yesterday the day I told Brother Lion that if he was n't careful, Mr. Man would catch him and put him in a cage for his children to look at. But he just hooted at it — and now, sure enough, there he is! I mind the first time he began his pursuit of Mr. Man. That was the time he got his hand caught in the split of the log."

"I done hear my daddy tell dat tale," remarked Drusilla.

"Yes," said Mr. Rabbit, "it soon became common talk in the neighborhood. Brother Lion had come a long way to hunt Mr. Man, and as soon as he got his hand out of the split in the log he started to go home again. I went part of the way with him, and then it was that I told him he'd find himself in a cage if he was n't careful. I made a burdock poultice for his hand the best I could — "

"And it's mighty good for bruises, I tell you now!" exclaimed Mrs. Meadows.

"And then Brother Lion went on home, feeling better, but still very mad. Crippled as he was, he was a quick traveler, and it was not long before he came to his journey's end.

"Well, when his mother saw him she was very

sorry. But when he told her what the matter
was she was vexed. 'Aha!' said she, 'how
often have I told you about meddling with somebody else's business! How often have I told
you about sticking your nose into things that
don't concern you! I'm not sorry for you one
bit, because if you had obeyed me you would n't
be coming home now with your hand mashed all
to flinders. But, no! daddy-like, you 've got to
go and get yourself into trouble with Mr. Man,
and now you see what has come of it. I 'm not
feeling at all well myself, but now I 've got to go
to work and make a whole parcel of poultices and
tie your hand up and nurse you — and I declare
somebody ought to be nursing me this very minute.'

"That was what Brother Lion's mother said,"
continued Mr. Rabbit, "but Brother Lion did n't
say anything. He just lay on the sheepskin
pallet she made him and studied how he would
be revenged on Mr. Man. After a while his
hand got well, but still he said very little about
the matter. The more he thought about the way
he had been treated, the madder he got. He
gnashed his teeth together and waved his long

tail about until it looked like a snake. Finally he sent word to all his kin — his uncles and his cousins — to meet him somewhere in the woods and hold a convention to consider how they should catch the great monster, Mr. Man, who had caused a log of wood to mash Brother Lion's hand.

"Well, it wasn't long before the uncles and cousins began to arrive. They came from far and near, and they seemed to be very ferocious. They shook their manes and showed their tushes. They went off in the woods and held their convention, and Brother Lion laid his complaint before them. He told them what kind of treatment he had received from Mr. Man, and asked them if they would help to get his revenge. He made quite a speech, and when he sat down, his uncles and cousins were very much excited. They roared and howled. They said they were ready to tear Mr. Man limb from limb. They declared they were ready to go where he was, and gnaw him and claw him on account of the scandalous way he had treated their blood-kin.

"But when Brother Lion's mother heard what they proposed to do she shut her eyes and shook

her head from side to side, and told the uncles
and the cousins that they had better go back
home, all of them. She said that before they
got through with Mr. Man they 'd wish they had
never been born. But go they would and go
they did.

"So they started out soon one morning, and
traveled night and day for nearly a week. They
were getting very tired and hungry, and some
of the younger blood-cousins wanted to stop and
rest, and some wanted to turn around and go
back home. But one morning while they were
going through the woods, feeling a little shaky
in head and limb, they suddenly came in sight of
Mr. Man. He was cutting down trees and split-
ting them into timber. He had his coat off, and
seemed to be very busy.

" But he was not so busy that he did n't hear
Mr. Lion and his uncles and blood-cousins sneak-
ing through the woods over the dry leaves, and
he was n't so busy that he could n't see them
moving about among the trees. He was very
much astonished. He wondered where so many
of the Lion family came from, and what they
were doing there, but he did n't stop to ask any

questions. He dropped his axe and climbed a tree.

"Brother Lion and his uncles and his blood-cousins were very much pleased when they saw Mr. Man climb the tree. 'We have him now,' said Brother Lion, and the rest licked their jaws and smiled. Then they gathered around the tree and sat on their haunches and watched Mr. Man. This didn't do any good, for Mr. Man sat on a limb and swung his legs, just as content-edly as if he was sitting in his rocking-chair at home.

"Then Brother Lion and his uncles and his blood-cousins showed their teeth and growled. But this didn't do any good. Mr. Man swung his feet and whistled a dance-tune. Then Brother Lion and his blood-cousins opened their mouths wide and roared as loud as they could. But this didn't do any good. Mr. Man leaned his head against the trunk of the tree and pre-tended to be nodding.

"This made Brother Lion and his blood-kin very mad. They ran around the tree and tore the bark with their claws, and waved their tails back and forth. But this didn't do any good.

Mr. Man just sat up there and swung his feet and laughed at them.

"Brother Lion and his blood-kin soon found that if they intended to capture Mr. Man they'd have to do something else besides caper around the foot of the tree. So they talked it over, and Brother Lion fixed up a plan. He said that he would stand at the foot of the tree and rear up against the trunk, and one of his blood-cousins could climb on his back and rear up, and then another cousin or uncle could climb up, and so on until there was a ladder of bloodthirsty Lions high enough to reach Mr. Man.

"Brother Lion, mind you, was to be at the bottom of the Lion ladder," remarked Mr. Rabbit, with a chuckle, "and he had a very good reason for it. He had had dealings with Mr. Man, and he wanted to keep as far away from him as possible. But before they made the Lion ladder, Brother Lion looked up at Mr. Man and called out : —

"'What are you doing up there?'

"'You'll find out a great deal too soon for your comfort,' replied Mr. Man.

"Brother Lion said, 'Come down from there.'

"Mr. Man answered, 'I'll come down much sooner than you want me to.'

"Then Brother Lion, his uncles, and his blood-cousins began to build their ladder. Brother Lion was the bottom round of this ladder, as you may say," continued Mr. Rabbit. "He reared up and placed his hands against the tree, and one of his uncles jumped on his shoulders, and put his hands against the tree. Then a cousin, and then another uncle, and so on until the ladder reached a considerable distance up the tree. It was such a high ladder that it began to wobble, and the last uncle had hard work to make his way to the top. He climbed up very carefully and slowly, for he was not used to this sort of business. He was the oldest and the fiercest of the old company, but his knees shook under him as he climbed up and felt the ladder shaking and wobbling.

"Mr. Man saw that by the time this big Lion got to the top of the ladder his teeth and his claws would be too close for comfort, and so he called out in an angry tone : —

"'Just hold on! Just stand right still! Wait! I'm not after any of you except that fellow at

the bottom there. I'm not trying to catch any
of you but him. He has bothered me before.
I let him go once, but I'll not let him get away
this time. Just stand right still and hold him
there till I climb down the other side of the
tree.'

"With that Mr. Man shook the limbs and
leaves and dropped some pieces of bark. This
was more than Brother Lion could stand. He
was so frightened that he jumped from under the
ladder, and his uncles and his blood-cousins came
tumbling to the ground, howling, growling, and
fighting.

"They were as sorry-looking a sight as ever
you saw when they came to their senses. Those
that didn't have their bones broken by the fall
were torn and mangled. They had acted so
foolishly that out of the whole number, Mr.
Man didn't get but three lion-skins that could be
called perfect.

"Brother Lion went home to his mother as
fast as he could go and remained quiet a long
time. And now you tell me he's in a cage."

Mr. Rabbit paused and shook his head until
his ears flopped.

D363271

The children seemed to enjoy the story very much; so much so, indeed, that Mrs. Meadows wanted Mr. Rabbit to tell some of his own queer experiences, but Mr. Rabbit laughed and said that it did n't seem exactly right to be telling his own stories. He said if he told the stories just as they happened, he 'd have to talk about himself a good deal, and people would think he was boastful. He declared he did n't feel like making his young friends think he was bragging.

"Oh, we shan't mind that," said Sweetest Susan, "shall we, brother?"

"Why, of course not," replied Buster John.

"La! we all done hear folks brag, till we got hardened ter braggin'!" exclaimed Drusilla.

So the children, aided by Mrs. Meadows, coaxed Mr. Rabbit until he finally consented to tell some of his queer adventures.

VIII.

Mr. Rabbit moved his body uneasily about, and scratched his head, and crossed and uncrossed his legs several times before he began.

" I declare it is n't right!" he exclaimed after a while. " I don't mind telling about other folks, but when it comes to talking about myself, it is a different thing."

" Don't you remember the time you tried to get Brother Terrapin to give you a fiddle-string ? " asked Mrs. Meadows, laughing a little.

" Oh, that was just a joke," replied Mr. Rabbit.

"Call it a joke, then," said Mrs. Meadows. " You know what the little boy said when the man asked him his name. He said, says he, ' You may call it anything, so you call me to dinner.' "

" He was n't very polite," remarked Sweetest Susan.

"No, indeed," Mrs. Meadows answered; "but you know that little boys can't always remember to be polite."

"I think we were at your house," suggested Mr. Rabbit, rubbing his chin.

"Yes," replied Mrs. Meadows. "In the little house by the creek. The yard sloped from the front door right to the bank."

"To be sure," exclaimed Mr. Rabbit, brightening up. "I remember the house just as well as if I had seen it yesterday. There was a little shelf on the left-hand side of the door as you came out, and there the water-bucket sat."

"Yes," said Mrs. Meadows; "and there was just room enough up there by the bucket for Brother Terrapin."

"That's so," Mr. Rabbit replied, laughing, "and when he used to go to your house to see the girls they'd set the bucket on the table in the house and lift Brother Terrapin to the shelf so he could see and be seen. I remember it used to make him very mad when I'd tell him he would be a mighty man if he wasn't so flat-footed."

"Oh, you used to talk worse than that," cried Mrs. Meadows, laughing heartily at the remembrance of it. "You used to tell him he was the only man you ever saw that sat down when he stood up. I declare! Brother Terrapin's eyes used to get right red."

"Well," said Mr. Rabbit, after a pause; "I remember I went to your house one day and I carried my fiddle. When I got there, who should I see but old Brother Terrapin sitting up on the shelf. I expected to find the girls by themselves, but there was Brother Terrapin. So I began to joke him.

"'Howdy, Brother Terrapin?' says I. 'If you had a ladder handy you could come downstairs and shake hands, couldn't you?'

"He began to get sullen and sulky at once. He wouldn't hardly make any reply. But I didn't care for that. Says I: 'Cross your legs and look comfortable, Brother Terrapin; don't be glum in company. I've got my fiddle with me, and I'm going to make your bones ache if you don't dance.'

"Then I whirled in," said Mr. Rabbit, "and played the liveliest tunes I could think of.— 'Billy in the Low Grounds,' ''Possum up the Gum-Stump,' 'Chicken in the Bread-Tray,' and all those hoppery-skippery, jiggery-dancery tunes that make your feet go whether or no. But there Brother Terrapin sat, looking as unconcerned as if the fiddle had been ten miles away. He did n't even keep time to the music with his foot. More than that, he did n't even wag his head from side to side."

"I always knew Brother Terrapin had no ear for music," remarked Mrs. Meadows. "If that was a fault, he certainly had more than his share of it."

"I ought not to talk about people behind their backs," Mr. Rabbit continued, trying to shake a fly out of his ear, "but I must say that Brother Terrapin was very dull about some things. Well, I played and played, and the girls danced and seemed to enjoy it. I believe you danced a round or two yourself?" Mr. Rabbit turned to Mrs. Meadows inquiringly.

"I expect I shook my foot a little," said Mrs. Meadows with a sigh. "I was none too good."

"They danced and danced until they were tired of dancing," Mr. Rabbit resumed; "but there sat Brother Terrapin as quiet as if he were asleep. Well, I was vexed — I don't mind say-

ing so now — I was certainly vexed. But I did n't let on. And between tunes I did my best to worry Brother Terrapin.

" ' Ladies,' says I, ' don't make so much fuss. Let Brother Terrapin get his nap out. You 'll turn a chair over directly, and Brother Terrapin will give a jump and fall off the shelf and break some of the furniture in his house.' This made the girls laugh very much, for they remembered the old saying that Brother Terrapin carries his house on his back. ' Don't laugh so loud,' says I, ' Brother Terrapin has earned his rest. He 's been courting on the other side of the creek, and he has no carriage to ride in when he goes back and forth. Sh-h ! ' says I, ' don't disturb him. When a person sits down when he stands up, and lies down when he walks, some allowance must be made.'

" Brother Terrapin's eyes grew redder and redder, and the skin on the back of his head began to work backward and forward. What might have happened I don't know, but just as the girls were in the middle of a dance one of my fiddle-strings broke, and it was the treble, too. I would n't have minded it if it had been any of

the other strings, but when the treble broke I had
to stop playing.

"Well, the girls were very much disappointed
and so was I, for I had come for a frolic. I
searched in my pockets, but I had no other string.
I tried to play with three strings, but the tune
would n't come. The girls were so sorry they
did n't know what to do.

"Just then an idea struck me. 'Ladies,' says
I, 'it 's a thousand pities I did n't bring an extra
treble, and I 'm perfectly willing to go home and
fetch one, but if Brother Terrapin was a little
more accommodating the music could go right on.
You could be dancing again in a little or no time.'

"'Oh, is that so?' says the girls. 'Well, we
know Brother Terrapin will oblige us.'

"'I 'm not so sure of that,' says I.

"'What do you want me to do?' says he. His
voice sounded as if he had the croup.

"'Ladies,' says I, 'you may believe it or not,
but if Brother Terrapin has a mind to he can lend
me a treble string that will just fit my fiddle.'

"'Brother Rabbit,' says he, 'you know I have
no fiddle-string. What would I be doing with
one?'

"'Don't mind him, ladies. He knows just as well as I do that he has a fiddle-string in his neck. I can take my pocket-knife and get it out in half a minute,' says I.

"This made Brother Terrapin roll his eyes.

"'Be ashamed of yourself, Brother Terrapin,' says the girls. 'And we were having so much fun, too.'

"'If my neck was as long and as tough as Brother Terrapin's, I'd take one of the leaders out and make a fiddle-string of it, just to oblige the ladies,' says I.

"The girls turned up their noses and tossed their heads. 'Don't pester Brother Terrapin,' says they. 'We'll not ask him any more.'

"'Ladies,' says I, 'there is a way to get the fiddle-string without asking for it. Will you please hand me a case-knife out of the cupboard there?'

"I rose from my chair with a sort of a frown," continued Mr. Rabbit, laughing heartily, "but before I could lift my hand Brother Terrapin rolled from the shelf and went tumbling down the slope to the creek, heels over head."

"Did it hurt him much?" asked Sweetest Susan, with a touch of sympathy.

"It did n't stop his tongue," replied Mr. Rabbit. "He crawled out on the other side of the creek and said very bad words. He even went so far as to call me out of my name. But it is all over with now," said Mr. Rabbit, with a sigh. "I bear no grudges. Let bygones be bygones."

"I never heard before that Brother Terrapin had a fiddle-string in his neck," said Buster John, after he had thought the matter over a little.

"In dem times," said Drusilla, as if to satisfy her own mind, "you could n't tell what nobody had skacely."

"Why, as to that," replied Mr. Rabbit, "the fiddle-string in his neck was news to Brother Terrapin."

There was a pause here and the children seemed to be somewhat listless.

"I'll tell you what I think," remarked Mrs. Meadows to Mr. Rabbit; "these children here are lonesome, and they'll be getting homesick long before the time comes for them to go. Oh, don't tell me!" she cried, when the children would have protested. "I know how I'd feel if I was away from home in a strange country and had nobody but queer people to talk to. We are

too old. Even Chickamy Crany Crow and Tickle-My-Toes are too old, and Mr. Thimblefinger is too little."

"Well, what are we going to do about it?" asked Mr. Rabbit, running his thumb in the bowl of his pipe.

"I was just thinking," responded Mrs. Meadows. "Had n't we better bring out the Looking-Glass family?"

"Well," said Mr. Rabbit, "I leave that to you." To hide the smile that gathered around his mouth Mr. Rabbit leaned his head over and scratched his left ear lazily with his left foot.

"That's what I'll do," Mrs. Meadows declared decisively. "These children want company they can appreciate, poor things!"

She went into the house, and presently came out again, bringing a mirror about three feet wide and five feet high.

IX.

THE LOOKING-GLASS CHILDREN.

THE frame of the mirror was of dark wood, curiously carved, and it was set on pivots between two small but stout upright posts, made of the same kind of wood. As Mrs. Meadows brought the looking-glass out, it swung back and forth between these posts, and its polished surface shone with great brilliancy. The children wondered how they were to amuse themselves with this queer toy. Mrs. Meadows placed the looking-glass a little way from them, but not facing them. The frame was in profile, so that they could see neither the face nor the back of the mirror.

"You come first," she said to Buster John.

He went forward, and Mrs. Meadows placed him in front of the looking-glass. As he turned to face it, his reflection (as it seemed) stepped from the mirror and stared at him. Buster John looked at Mrs. Meadows for an explanation, but at that moment she beckoned to Sweetest Susan.

When Buster John moved, his image moved. Mrs. Meadows pushed him gently aside to make room for Sweetest Susan, and it seemed that some invisible hand pushed his reflection gently aside.

Sweetest Susan stepped before the looking-glass, and her reflection walked out to meet her. Drusilla now came forward, and her image stepped forth, looking somewhat scared and showing the whites of its eyes. Mrs. Meadows went to the looking-glass, gave it a sudden turn on its pivots, and carried it into the house.

All this happened so rapidly that the children hardly had time to be surprised, but now that the looking-glass had been carried away and they were left with their reflections, their shadows, their images (or whatever it was), they didn't know what to do, or say, or think. They could only look at each other in dumb astonishment. Drusilla was the first to break the silence. In her surprise she had moved quickly back a few steps, and her image, which had come out of the looking-glass, had as quickly moved forward and toward her a few steps.

"Don't come follerin' atter me!" she cried excitedly. "Kaze ef you do, you'll sho' git hurted. I ain't done nothin' 't all ter you. I ain't gwine ter pester you, an' I ain't gwine ter let you pester me. I tell you dat now, so you'll know what ter 'pen' on."

"Don't move! Please don't move!" cried Sweetest Susan to Buster John. "If you do I can't tell you apart. I won't know which is which. That wouldn't be treating me right nor mamma, either."

Naturally, the children were in a great predicament when Mrs. Meadows came back. She saw the trouble at once, and began to laugh. It was funny to see Buster John and Sweetest Susan and Drusilla standing there staring first at the Looking-Glass children and then at themselves, not daring to move for fear they would get mixed up with their doubles. The Looking-Glass children stared likewise, first at themselves and then at the others.

"What is the matter?" Mrs. Meadows asked. "Why don't you go and play with one another and make friends? It isn't many folks that have the chance you children have got."

"I don't feel like playing," said Sweetest

Susan. " I 'm afraid we 'll get mixed up so that nobody will know one from the other."

" Why, there 's all the difference in the world," exclaimed Mrs. Meadows, trying hard not to laugh. " The Looking-Glass children are all left-handed. You have a flower on the left side of your hat, the other Susan has a flower on the right side of hers. Your brother there has buttons on the right side of his coat; the other John has buttons on the left side. There is a flaw in the looking-glass, and Drusilla, being a little taller than you two, was just tall enough for the end of her nose to be even with the flaw. That 's the reason the other Drusilla's nose looks like it had been mashed with a hammer."

" Yes 'm, it do ! " exclaimed Drusilla. She involuntarily took a step forward to take a nearer view of the flawed nose, and of course the other Drusilla took a step forward as if to show the flawed nose. " Don't you dast ter come 'bout me ! " exclaimed Drusilla. " Goodness knows, I don't look dat away. Go on, now ! Go 'ten' ter yo' own business ef you got any."

" I don't want to play with you," said the other

Drusilla. "You've got smut on your face. I don't like to play with dirty-faced girls."

"My face cleaner'n yone dis blessed minnit," retorted Drusilla.

"And your hair is not combed," said the other Drusilla. "It is wrapped with strings, and you couldn't comb it if you wanted to. I think it is a shame."

"Look at yo' own head!" retorted Drusilla angrily. "It's mo' woolly dan what mine is. 'T ain't never been kyarded much less combed. An' who got any mo' strings roun' der hair dan you got on yone?"

"How could I help it?" the other Drusilla asked. "You came and looked at me in the glass and I had to be just like you, smutty face and all. I don't think it is right. I know I never looked like this before, and I hope I never shall again."

"Tut, tut!" said Mrs. Meadows; "don't get to mooning around here. You might look better, but you don't look so bad. It will all come right on wash-day, as the woman said when she put her dress on wrong side outwards. Here comes Chickamy Crany Crow and Tickle-My-Toes. They'll be glad to see you, no matter how you look."

And they were. They ran to the Looking-Glass children and greeted them warmly. Tickle-My-Toes stared at the other Drusilla in surprise, but he did n't laugh at her. " You look as if you had fallen down the chimney," he said, " but that does n't make any difference. So long as you are here, we are satisfied."

" Oh, I don't mind it," said the other Drusilla.

" Now, then," remarked Mrs. Meadows, " you could n't please us better than to sing us a song. You have n't practiced together for a long time."

The other children looked at one another in a shamefaced way, and then, without a word of objection or explanation, they began to sing as with one voice, the most plaintive song that ever was heard. It may be called : —

THE LOOKING-GLASS SONG.

It 's oh ! and it 's ah ! It 's alack ! and alas !
Just imagine you lived in a big looking-glass !

Oh, what could you say and what could you do
If you lived all alone in the toe of a shoe ?
You could hop, you could skip, you could jump, you could dance,
And you 'd hear very little of " should n'ts " and " shan'ts."
You could stump your big toe, and it would never get hurt ;
You could kick up the sand, you could play in the dirt.

But it 's oh ! and it 's ah !   It 's alack ! and alas !
Just imagine you lived in a big looking-glass !

Oh, what could you do, and what would you say
If you lived in the pantry all night and all day ?
You could say it was jolly, and splendid, and nice ;
You could eat all the jelly, and frighten the mice.
You could taste the preserves, you could nibble the cheese —
You could smell the red pepper, and sit down and sneeze.

But it 's oh ! and it 's ah !   It 's alack ! and alas !
Just imagine you lived in a big looking-glass !

Oh, what could you do if you lived under ground ?
You could ride Mr. Mole and go galloping round ;
You could hear the black cricket a-playing his fife,
For to quiet the baby and please his dear wife.
You could hear the green grasshopper frying his meat,
Near the nest of the June-Bug under the wheat.
You could get all the goobers and artichokes, too —
You could peep from the window the grub-worm went through.

But it 's oh ! and it 's ah !   It 's alack ! and alas !
Just imagine you lived in a big looking-glass !

"Oh, I think that is splendid," cried Sweetest
Susan.

"Mr. Rabbit does n't like it much," replied
Mrs. Meadows, "but I tell him it is pretty good
for children that were raised in a Looking-Glass."

"It will do very well," remarked Mr. Rabbit,

" but you 'll hear nicer songs by the time you are
as old as I am."

" Dem ar white chillun done mighty well,"
said Drusilla, " but I don't like de way dat ar nigger gal hilt her head."

" Do they have to stay in the looking-glass ? "
asked Buster John. " If they do I 'm sorry for
them."

" I ain't sorry fer dat black gal," said Drusilla
spitefully. " She too ugly ter suit me."

" Whose fault is it but yours ? " cried Chickamy
Crany Crow.

" Yes, whose fault is it ? " cried Tickle-My-Toes.

" Come, come ! " cries Mrs. Meadows. " We
want no trouble here."

" We 'll not trouble her," answered Tickle-My-
Toes. " Old Rawhead-and-Bloody-Bones will do
the troubling."

" Now you all heah dat ! " exclaimed Drusilla,
in some alarm. " I ain't pesterin' nobody, an' I
ain't doin' nothin' 't all. If I can't talk I des ez
well quit livin'. I 'm gwine home, I am, an' ef I
can't fin' de way, den I 'll know who 'll have ter
answer fer it."

" Well, if you go," said Mrs. Meadows, " you 'll

have company. The other black girl will have to go too."

" How come dat?" exclaimed Drusilla.

" It would take me too long to tell you," replied Mrs. Meadows. " Why does your shadow in a looking-glass make every motion that you make? Because it's obliged to — that's all. That's just the reason the other black girl would follow you."

" Don't mind Drusilla," said Buster John. "She just talks to hear herself talk. Her mouth flies open before she knows it."

" Well, the poor things won't trouble you long," said Mrs. Meadows. " They'll want to go back home presently."

" Do they have to stay in the looking-glass?" inquired Buster John, repeating a question he had already asked.

" Well, they were born and raised there," replied Mrs. Meadows. " It is their home, and, although they are glad to get out for a little while, they wouldn't be very happy if they had to stay out."

The children and the Looking-Glass children played together a little while, or made believe to

play, but they did n't seem to enjoy themselves.
Mrs. Meadows noticed this and asked Mr. Rabbit
the reason.

"Simple enough, simple enough," Mr. Rabbit
answered. "They are so much alike in their
looks and ways and so different in their raising
that they can't get on together. How would I
feel if my double were to walk out of the side of
the house and sit here facing me and mimicking
my every motion? I would n't feel very comfortable, I can tell you."

"I reckon not," said Mrs. Meadows. Presently she called the children, brought out the
looking-glass and told them it was time to bid the
others good-by. At this the other children seemed
to be very well pleased. The other Buster John
and the other Sweetest Susan shook hands all
round, and the other Drusilla made a curtsey
to the company. Then, with a run and a jump,
they plunged into the big looking-glass as you
have seen youngsters plunge into a pond of water.

"Ho!" cried Mr. Thimblefinger, "they jumped
in with a splash, but they never made a ripple."

"They have n't room enough in there to turn
around," said Sweetest Susan.

"Why not?" inquired Mr. Thimblefinger. "To them the world is a looking-glass, and a mighty little one at that. If you were to peep in their glass now they'd peep back at you; but, as they look at it, you are in a looking-glass and they are out of it. And I wouldn't be surprised if they are a great deal sorrier for you than you are for them."

"When are we to go home?" asked Sweetest Susan plaintively.

"Oho! you want to get back into your looking-glass!" cried Mr. Thimblefinger merrily. "Well, you won't have long to wait. By rights, you ought to stay here twelve hours, but the old Spring Lizard and I have put our heads together, and we've fixed it so that you can get back before sundown."

"Isn't it night at home now?" inquired Buster John.

"Why, they are hardly through washing the dinner dishes," replied Mrs. Meadows.

"It is just half past two," said Mr. Thimblefinger, looking at his watch.

"Well, it look so dark all dis time dat I done got hungry fer supper," remarked Drusilla.

X.

MR. RABBIT AS A RAIN-MAKER.

"I HOPE it won't rain," said Sweetest Susan, "for then the spring would fill up so we couldn't get out, and we should get wet down here."

"Oh, no," replied Mr. Thimblefinger, "the water is never wet down here. It is a little damp, that's all."

"Well, that's enough, I'm sure," remarked Mr. Rabbit. "It's enough to give me the wheezes when I first get up in the morning, and it's not at all comfortable, I can tell you."

"There is one funny thing about springs," said Mrs. Meadows, "no matter how much it rains, they never get any fuller. They may run a little freer, but they never get any fuller. Speaking of rains," she continued, turning to Mr. Rabbit and laughing, "don't you remember the time you set yourself up as a rain-maker?"

Mr. Rabbit chuckled so that he bent nearly double.

"I don't remember that," sighed Mr. Thimble-finger. "You two have more jokes between you than you can shake a stick at. That comes of me being small and puny. Tell us about it, please."

Mr. Rabbit fingered his pipe — a way he had when he put on his thinking-cap, as Mrs. Meadows expressed it — and presently said : —

"It's not such a joke after all, but I'll let you judge for yourself. Once upon a time, when all of us lived next door, on the other side of the spring, there was a tremendous drouth. I had been living a long time, but never before had seen such a long dry spell. Everybody was farming except myself, and even I had planted a small garden.

"Well, there was a big rain about planting-time, but after that came the drouth, and the hot weather with it. One month, six weeks, two months, ten weeks — and still no sign of rain. The cotton was all shriveled up, and the corn looked as if it would catch a-fire, it was so dry; even the cow-peas turned yellow. Everything was parched. The creeks ran dry, and the rivers got so low the mills had to stop. I remember

that when Brother Bear tried to carry me across
the ferry his flatboat ran aground in the middle
of the river, and the water was so low we found
we could wade out.

"The drouth got so bad that everybody was
complaining — everybody except me. Brother
Wolf and Brother Bear would come and sit on
my front porch and do nothing but complain ;
but I said nothing. I simply smoked my pipe
and shook my head, and said nothing. They noticed this, after so long a time, and one day. while
they were sitting there complaining and declaring
that they were ruined, I went in to get a drink
of water. I came back gently and heard them
asking each other how it was that I did n't join
in their complaints. When I came out, Brother
Wolf says, says he : 'Brother Rabbit, how are
your craps?' I remember he said 'craps.'

" 'Well,' says I, 'my craps are middling good.
They might be better, and they might be worse,
but I have no cause to grumble.'

"They looked at each other, and then Brother
Bear asked if I had had any rain at my house.
'None,' says I, 'to brag about — a drizzle here
and a drizzle there, but nothing to boast of.'

"They looked at each other in great surprise, and then Brother Wolf spoke up. 'Brother Rabbit,' says he, 'how can you get a drizzle and the rest of us not a drop?'

"'Well,' says I, 'some folks that know me call me the rain-maker. They may be right. They may be wrong. I'm not going to squabble about it. You can call me what you please. I shall not dispute with you.'

"Presently they went away, but it was n't long before they came back, bringing with them all the neighbors for miles around. They gathered in the porch and in the yard and outside the gate, and begged me, if I was a rain-maker, to make it rain there and then to save their crops. They begged me and begged me, but I sat cross-legged and smoked my pipe — this same pipe you see here. Brother Fox, who had done me many a mean trick (though he was always well paid for it), got on his knees and begged me to make it rain for them.

"Finally I told them that I 'd make it rain for the whole settlement on two conditions. The first condition was that every one was to pay toll."

"Toll is the pay the miller takes out at the mill," remarked Buster John.

"Yes," replied Mr. Rabbit, "you take your turn of meal to the mill and the miller takes his payment out of the meal. Well, I told them they'd have to pay toll. They agreed to that, and then asked what else they'd have to do, but I said we'd attend to one thing at a time. First let the toll be paid.

"They went off, and in due time they came back. Some brought corn and some brought meal; some brought wheat and some brought flour; some brought milk and some brought butter; some brought honey in the clean, and some brought honey in the comb; some brought one thing and some brought another, but they all brought something.

"Then they gathered around and asked what else they had to do. 'Well,' says I, 'you certainly act as if you wanted rain — all of you — there's no disputing that. You have paid the toll according to agreement. You have surely earned the rain, and now there's nothing for me to do but to find out how much rain you want.'

"With that they all began to talk at once, especially Brother Bear, who lived in the upland district, where the drouth had been the worst, but I put an end to that at once.

" 'Hold on there!' says I, 'just wait! Don't get into any dispute around here. You are on my grounds and at my house. Let's have no squabbling. I'm not feeling so mighty well, anyhow, and the least fuss will be enough to upset me. But the world is wide. Just go on yonder hill and fix up the whole matter to suit yourselves. Just come to some agreement as to how much rain you want, and as soon as you agree send me word, and then go home and hoist your parasols, for there'll surely be a sprinkle.'

"Well," Mr. Rabbit continued, " this was such a sensible plan that they couldn't help but agree to it, and presently they all went to the hill and began to talk the matter over, while I went into the house.

"This was in the morning. Well, dinner-time came, but still no word had come from the convention on the hill. I went out into the porch, flung my red handkerchief over my face to keep the flies off, and took my afternoon nap, but still no word came from the hill. Then I fell to laughing, and laughed until I nearly choked myself."

"But what were you laughing at?" Buster John inquired, with a serious air.

Mr. Rabbit paused, looked at the youngster solemnly, and said, "Well, I'll tell you. I didn't laugh because anybody had hurt my feelings. I just laughed at circumstances. I sat and waited until the afternoon was half gone, and then slipped up the hill to see what was to be seen and hear what was to be heard. Everything was very quiet up there. Those who had gone up there to decide what sort of rain they wanted were sitting around under the pine-trees, looking very sour and saying nothing. The ground was torn up a little in spots, and I thought I could see scattered around little patches of hair and little pieces of hide. I judged from that that the arguments they had used were very serious. I watched them from behind the bushes a little while, and then Brother Bear walked out into the open and declared that any one who didn't want the rain to be a trash-mover was anything but a nice fellow. At this Brother Coon, who lived in the low grounds, remarked that anybody who wanted anything more than a drizzle was not well raised at all.

"Then I soon found out what the trouble was. Brother Bear, living on the uplands, wanted a big rain; Brother Coon, who lived in the low grounds, wanted a little rain; Brother Fox wanted a tolerably heavy shower; and Brother Mink just wanted a cloudy night to coax the frogs out. Some wanted a freshet, some wanted a drizzle, and some wanted a fog.

"They wouldn't agree because they couldn't agree," continued Brother Rabbit, "and finally they slunk off to their homes one at a time. So I didn't have to make any rain at all."

"But you couldn't have made it rain," said Sweetest Susan placidly.

"I didn't say I could," replied Mr. Rabbit. "I told them I would make the rain if they would agree among themselves."

"But you took what they brought you?" suggested Sweetest Susan in a tone that was intended for a rebuke.

"Well," Mr. Rabbit answered, "you know what the old saying is — 'Fools have to pay for

their folly.' They might as well have paid me as
to pay somebody else. That's the way I looked
at it in those days. I don't know how I'd look
at it now, because I'm not so nimble footed as I
used to be, nor so full of mischief."

"If there had been many more such fools in
your neighborhood," remarked Mr. Thimblefinger, " you could have set up a grocery-store."

There was a little pause, and then Mrs. Meadows, looking around, exclaimed : —

" Just look yonder, will you ? "

Chickamy Crany Crow had two sticks, and with
these she was playing on an imaginary fiddle.
Tickle-My-Toes had the broom, and this, he pretended, was a banjo.

The two queer-looking creatures wagged their
heads from side to side and patted the ground
with their feet, just as though they were making
sure-enough music, and presently Tickle-My-Toes
sang this song to a very lively tune : —

OH, LULLYMALOO !

I'll up and I'll grin if you tickle my chin,
And I'll sneeze if you tickle my nose ;
I'll up and I'll cry if you tickle my eye —
But I'll squeal if you tickle my toes !

Oh, grin with your chinnery in,
  And sneeze with your nosery oze,
And cry with your wipery eye,
  But please don't tickle my toes !

I 'll grin and I 'll sneeze, I 'll cry and I 'll squeal,
  And scare you with *ouches!* and *ohs !*
You may tickle my head, you may tickle my heel,
  But please don't tickle my toes !

Oh, grin with your innery chin,
  And sneeze with your ozery nose,
And cry with your wipery eye,
  But please don't tickle my toes !

I 'll grin, *tee-hee !* and I 'll cry, *boo-hoo!*
  And I 'll sneeze, *icky chow !* *icky-chose !*
And I 'll squeal just as loud, *Oh, Lullymaloo!*
  Whenever you tickle my toes ! "

Buster John, Sweetest Susan, and Drusilla
laughed so heartily at this that Chickamy Crany
Crow and Tickle-My-Toes did n't wait to repeat
the chorus of the song, but ran away, pretending
to be very much frightened. This made the
children laugh still more, and for the first time
they felt thoroughly at home in Mr. Thimblefinger's queer country.

XI.

HOW BROTHER BEAR'S HAIR WAS COMBED.

WHILE Buster John, Sweetest Susan, and Drusilla were watching Chickamy Crany Crow and Tickle-My-Toes run away, and laughing at them, suddenly the sky in Mr. Thimblefinger's queer country grew brighter. The dark shadow of the buttermilk-jug had disappeared, and there were wavering lines of white light flashing across, as though the sun were trying to shine through. Along with these flashing lines there were wavering lines of shadow that rippled and danced about curiously. There seemed to be some tremendous commotion going on. If some person with the learning and wisdom of an astronomer had seen this wonderful display, he would have been overcome with awe and fear. He would have concluded that the sky was about to go to pieces, and ten to one he would have left his unreflecting telescope swinging in the air, and crawled under the bed.

But there was no astronomer in Mr. Thimble-finger's queer country, and the children had seen too many strange sights to be very much alarmed. Besides, Drusilla solved the mystery before they had time to gather their fears together.

"Shuh!" she exclaimed; "'t ain't nothin' 't all. When dey tuck de jug outin' de spring de water 'bleedge to be shuck up."

And it was true. The rippling and wavering in the sky of Mr. Thimblefinger's queer country were caused by lifting the buttermilk-jug from the spring. As soon as the commotion ceased, it was seen that across the sky, from horizon to horizon, dark lines and shadows extended. They were irregular, and branched out here and there in every direction. Drusilla gazed at them for some moments without venturing to explain them. Suddenly a shadow that seemed to have life and motion made its appearance, and darted about among the dark lines. Drusilla laughed.

"La! Hit's dat dead lim' ober de spring, an' dere's a jay-bird hoppin' about in it right now. Ain't I done heah yo' pa say dat lim' 'll hafter be cut off 'fo' it fall an' break somebody's head?"

"Well, well! She ain't so bad off up here as

I thought she was," said Mr. Thimblefinger, tapping his forehead significantly.

" Ain't I done tell you dat dey's mo' in my head dan what you kin comb out?" exclaimed Drusilla indignantly.

" Speaking of combing and things of that sort," remarked Mr. Rabbit, turning to Mrs. Meadows, " did I ever tell you how Brother Bear learned to comb his hair?"

Mrs. Meadows reflected a moment, or pretended to reflect. " Now, I'm not right certain about that. Maybe you have and maybe you haven't; I don't remember. How did you teach Brother Bear to keep his hair roached and parted? Mostly when I used to know him, he went about looking mighty ragged and shabby."

Mr. Rabbit chuckled for several moments and then said: " Well, in my courting-days, you know, I used to go around fixed up in style. Many and many a time I've heard the girls whisper to one another and say, ' Oh, my! Ain't Mr. Rabbit looking spruce to-day?' There was one season in particular that I was careful to primp up and look sassy. I put bergamot oil on my hair, and kept it brushed so slick that a

fly would slip up and cripple himself if he lit
on it.

"It so happened that my road took me by Brother Bear's house every day — right by the front
gate. Sometimes Mrs. Bear would be hanging
out clothes on the fence, sometimes she would be
sweeping off the front porch, and sometimes she
would be working in the garden; but no matter
what she was doing I'd cough and catch her eye,
and then I'd bow just as polite as you please."

"What were you doing all that for?" asked
Buster John.

"Well, I'll tell you," Mr. Rabbit replied. "I
had a grudge against Brother Bear, and I wanted
to work a little scheme. Along at first I just
went on by the back of Brother Bear's house,
and around through the woods home, but in a
few days I'd pass by the house and then get over
the fence and creep back to hear what Mrs. Bear
had to say. One morning I heard her talking.
She was out in the yard fixing to do her week's
washing while Brother Bear was in the house
dozing. I could hear what Mrs. Bear said, but I
was too far off to hear what answer Brother Bear
made.

"Mrs. Bear says, says she: 'Honey, you ain't asleep, are you? Brother Rabbit has just gone along by the gate dressed to kill.' A grumbling sound came from the house. Mrs. Bear says, says she, 'I wonder where he goes every day, with his hair combed so slick?' Grumble in the house. 'You'd better wish you looked half as nice,' says Mrs. Bear. Grumble in the house. 'Well, I don't care if he is a grand rascal, he looks nice and clean, and that's more than anybody can say about you,' says Mrs. Bear. Growl in the house. Mrs. Bear says, says she, 'Oh, you can rip and rear, but Brother Rabbit goes about with his head combed, and he looks lots better that way than them that go about with rat nests in their hair — lots better.'"

Here Brother Rabbit chuckled again. "I thought to myself, thinks I, that I'd better be getting on toward home, and so I crept back up the fence and went on my way.

"The next day as I was going along the road, who should I meet but old Brother Bear himself. Well, here's a row, thinks I, but it did n't turn out so. Brother Bear was just as polite to me as I had been to his old woman.

" We passed the time of day and talked about the crops a little while, but I could see that Brother Bear had something serious on his mind. Finally, he shuffled around and sat down on a stump beside the roadside.

" ' Brother Rabbit,' he says, says he, ' how in the world do you manage to keep your hair so slick and smooth all the time ? My old woman sees you passing by every day, and she 's been worrying the life out of me because I don't keep my hair combed that way. So I said to myself I 'd ask you the very next time I met you.'

" Brother Bear was looking pretty rough and tough, and so I says, says I, ' You look as if she had been tousling you about it.'

" He hung his head at this, and shuffled around and changed his seat. Says he : ' No, it 's not so bad as all that, but I want to ask you plump and plain, if it 's a fair question, how you comb your hair so it will stay nice ? '

" I looked at him and shook my head. Says I, ' Brother Bear, I don't comb my hair.'

" He was so much surprised that he opened his mouth, and his tongue hung out on one side — a big, red tongue that had known the taste of innocent blood. "

"That's the truth!" exclaimed Mrs. Meadows. Sweetest Susan shuddered.

"Says he, 'Brother Rabbit, if you don't comb your hair, how in the wide world do you keep it so smooth?'

"Says I, 'Easy enough. Every morning my old woman takes the axe and chops my head off—'"

"Oh!" cried Sweetest Susan.

"'Takes the axe and chops off my head,'" Mr. Rabbit continued, as solemn as a judge, "'and carries it out in the yard, where she can have light to see and room to work, and then she combs it and combs it until every kink comes straight and every hair is in its place. Then she brings my head back, puts it where it belongs, and there it is — all combed.'

"Brother Bear seemed to be very much astonished. Says he, 'Doesn't it hurt, Brother Rabbit?'

"Says I, 'Hurt who? I'm no chicken.'

"Says he, 'Doesn't it bleed?'

"Says I, 'No more than enough to make my appetite good.'"

Mr. Rabbit paused and looked up at the ripples of light and shade that were chasing each other across the sky in Mr. Thimblefinger's queer country. Then he looked at the children.

"The upshot of it was," he continued, "that Brother Bear went home and told Mrs. Bear how I had my head combed every day. Woman-like, she wanted to try it at once; so Brother Bear laid his head on a log of wood, and Mrs. Bear got the axe and raised it high in the air. Brother Bear had just time to squall out, 'Cut it off easy, old woman!' when the axe fell on his neck, and there he was!"

"Oh, did it kill him?" cried Sweetest Susan.

"That's what the neighbors said," replied Mr. Rabbit placidly.

Sweetest Susan didn't seem to be at all pleased. Seeing this, Mrs. Meadows exclaimed: —

"To think of the poor little pigs Brother Bear killed and ate!"

"Yes," said Mr. Rabbit, "and the lambs!"

"Worse than that!" cried Mr. Thimblefinger. "Think of the little children he devoured! Think of it!"

"I'm glad he had his head cut off," said Buster John heartily.

"Me too, honey," assented Drusilla.

XII.

AFTER telling how Brother Bear learned to comb his hair, Mr. Rabbit closed his eyes and seemed to be about to fall into a doze, as old people have been known to do. During the pause that followed, Sweetest Susan saw what appeared to be a bird of peculiar shape sailing around in the sky of Mr. Thimblefinger's queer country.

It was long of body and seemed to have no wings, and yet it sailed about overhead as majestically and easily as an eagle could have done.

" What sort of a bird is it?" inquired Sweetest Susan, pointing out the object to Mrs. Meadows.

" Now, really, I don't know," was the reply. " They are so high in the sky and I've seen them so often that I've never bothered my head about them."

Mr. Thimblefinger climbed on the back of a chair, so as to get a better view of the curious bird, but he shook his head and climbed nimbly

down again. The queer bird was too much for
Mr. Thimblefinger. Mr. Rabbit opened his eyes
lazily and looked at it.

"If I 'm not much mistaken —" he started to
say, but Drusilla broke in without any cere-
mony : —

" 'T ain't nothin' 't all, but one er dem ar meller
bugs what swims roun' in de spring."

" Why, I expect it *is* a mellow bug," said Mrs.
Meadows, laughing. " I used to catch them
when I was a girl and put them in my handkerchief. They smell just like a ripe apple."

" I thought it was a buzzard," said Buster
John.

" No," remarked Mr. Rabbit, " I used to be
well acquainted with Brother Buzzard, and when
he 's in the air he 's longer from side to side than
he is from end to end. I don't know when I 've
thought of Brother Buzzard before. I never liked
him much, but I used to see him sailing around
on sunshiny days, or sitting in the top of a dead
pine drying his wings after a heavy rain. He
cut a very funny figure sitting up there, with
his wings spread out and drooping like a sick
chicken.

"I remember the time, too, when he had a singing-match with Brother Crow, and I nearly laughed myself to death over it."

"Oh, tell us about it," cried Buster John.

"There's nothing in it when it is told," replied Mr. Rabbit. "There are some things that are funny when you see them, but not funny at all when you come to tell about them."

"We don't mind that," said Sweetest Susan.

"I don't know exactly how it came about," resumed Mr. Rabbit, after a pause, "but as near as I can remember, Brother Buzzard and Brother Crow met with each other early one morning in a big pine-tree. They howdied, but there was a sort of coolness between them on account of the fact that Brother Buzzard had been going about the neighborhood making his brags and his boasts that he could outfly Brother Crow. They had n't been up in the tree very long before they began to dispute. Brother Buzzard was not a very loud talker in those days, whatever he may be now, but Brother Crow could squall louder than a woman who has been married twenty-two years. And so there they had it, quarreling and disputing and disturbing the peace."

"What were they quarreling about?" Buster John inquired.

"Well," replied Mr. Rabbit, "you know the road that leads to Brag is the shortest route to Bluster. Brother Buzzard and Brother Crow were quarreling because they had been bragging, and a little more and they'd have had a regular pitched battle then and there.

"'Maybe you can outfly me, Brother Buzzard,' says Mr. Crow, 'but I'll be bound you can't outsing me.'

"'I have never tried,' says Brother Buzzard, says he.

"'Well, suppose you try it now,' says Brother Crow. 'I'll go you a fine suit of clothes, and a cocked hat to boot, that I can sit here and sing longer than you can,' says he.

"'Oh, ho!' says Brother Buzzard, 'you may sing louder, but you can't sing longer than I can,' says he.

"'Is it a go?' says Brother Crow.

"'It's a go,' says Brother Buzzard, says he.

"'It's no fair bet,' says Brother Crow, 'because you are a bigger man than I am, and it stands to reason that you have got more wind in your craw than I have, but I shall give you one trial if I split my gizzard,' says he.

"Yes," remarked Mr. Rabbit, scratching his head thoughtfully, " those were the very words he used — 'if I split my gizzard,' says he. Well, they shook hands to ratify the bet, and then Brother Crow, without making any flourishes, raised the tune, —

> "'Oh, Susy, my Susy, gangloo !
> Oh, Milly, my Molly, langloo !'

" Then Brother Buzzard flung his head back and chimed in, —

> "'Oh, Susy, my Susy, gangloo !
> Oh, Milly, my Molly, langloo !'

and such another racket as they made I never heard before, and have never heard since."

"Why, what kind of a song was it?" inquired Sweetest Susan. "I'm sure I never heard such a song."

"Well," replied Mr. Rabbit, "you are young and I am old, but you know just as much about that song as I do, and maybe more than I do, for you haven't been pestered with it as long as I have. It is a worse riddle to me than it was the day I heard it."

"What did they do then?" asked Buster John.

"Well," Mr. Rabbit replied, "they sat there and sang just as I told you. Brother Buzzard would stop to catch his breath and then break out, —

> "'Oh. Susy, my Susy, gangloo !
> Oh, Milly, my Molly, langloo!'

and then Brother Crow would squall out, —

> "'Oh, Susy, my Susy, gangloo !'
> Oh, Milly, my Molly, langloo!'

"They sang on until they began to get hungry, and as Brother Buzzard seemed to be the biggest and fattest of the two, everybody thought he would hold out the longest. But Brother Crow was plucky, and he sang right along in spite of the emptiness in his craw. He didn't squall as loud as he did at first, but every time Brother Buzzard sang, Brother Crow would sing, too. By and by, they both began to get very weak.

"At last, as luck would have it, Brother Crow saw his wife flying over, and he sang out as loud as he could : —

"'Oh, Susy! — Go tell my children — my

Sissy, — to bring my dinner — gangloo! — and tell them — oh, Milly, my Molly, — to bring it quickly — langloo!'

"It was n't very long after that before all Brother Crow's family connections came flying to help him, and as soon as they found out how matters stood they brought him more victuals than he knew what to do with. Brother Buzzard held out as long as he could, but he was obliged to give up, and since that time there has been mighty little singing in the Buzzard family.

"But that is n't all," remarked Mr. Rabbit, as solemnly as if he were pointing a moral. "Since that time Brother Crow, who was dressed in white, has been wearing the black suit that he won from Brother Buzzard."

"Speaking of singing birds," said Mr. Thimblefinger, turning to Mrs. Meadows, "what is that song I used to hear you humming about a little bird?"

"Oh, it 's just a nonsense song," replied Mrs. Meadows. "It has no beginning and no ending.

But the children said they wanted to hear it, anyhow, and so Mrs. Meadows sang about —

THE LITTLE BIRD.

There was once a little Bird so full of Song
That he sang in the Rose-Bush the whole Night long.

And " Oh," said the Redbird to the Jay,
" Don't you wish you could sit and sing that way ? "
" Mercy, no ! " said the Jay ; " for he sings too late ;
I sing well enough for to please my Mate."

There was once a little Bird so full of Song
That he sang in the Rose-Bush the whole Night long.

Then " Oh," said the Redbird to the Crow,
" Don't you wish you could sit and sing just so ? "
" Do hush," said the Crow, " or I 'll start for to weep,
Be — caw — caw — cause he 's a-losing of his sleep."

There was once a little Bird so full of Song
That he sang in the Rose-Bush the whole Night long.

And " Oh," said the Redbird to the Wren,
" Don't you wish you could sing so now and then ? "
" Not me," said the Wren as she shook her Head ;
" I think his Mamma ought to put him to Bed."

But the Singing Bird was so full of Glee
That he sang all night in the Rose-Bush Tree.

XIII.

" Isn't it almost time for us to start home?" said Sweetest Susan, turning to Mr. Thimblefinger.

" Why, you've got all the afternoon before you," replied Mr. Thimblefinger. " Besides it will be downhill all the way. I was just going to tell you a story, but if you really want to go I'll put off the telling of it until some of your grandchildren tumble in the spring when the wet water has run out and the dry water has taken its place."

" Tell the story, please," said Buster John.

" It's about a girl," remarked Mr. Thimblefinger. " She was called the Strawberry-Girl. My mother knew the girl well, and I've heard her tell the story many a time. But if you want to go home — "

" Oh, please tell the story," cried Sweetest Susan.

"Well," said Mr. Thimblefinger; "once there was an old woman who lived in the woods. She lived all alone, and people said she was a witch. She was so old that the skin on her forehead had deep wrinkles in it, and these wrinkles caused everybody to think that the old woman was frowning all the time. People called her Granny Grim-Eye.

"Whenever Granny Grim-Eye got hungry she went to a strawberry-patch in the field near where she lived, and gathered a basket of strawberries. One day when she went after strawberries she found a beautiful little girl asleep in the patch.

"'Hity-tity!' said Granny Grim-Eye, 'what are you doing here? Where did you come from, and where are you going?'

"The little girl awoke and stared at Granny Grim-Eye. She was tied to a blackberry-bush by a silver chain so fine that the links of it could hardly be seen with the naked eye. 'Who are you?' asked Granny Grim-Eye.

"'Nothing nor nobody,' replied the little girl, and that was all the answer Granny Grim-Eye could get from the child.

"'Well,' said Granny Grim-Eye, 'this is my strawberry-patch, and everything I find in it belongs to me. I'll take you home and see what I can make out of you.'

"So she took the girl home and cared for her, giving her the name of the Strawberry-Girl. In the course of time the Strawberry-Girl grew to be the most beautiful young woman in the country, but her mind was not bright. In fact, I have heard my mother say that the Strawberry-Girl was as stupid and as silly as she could be, but she was so beautiful that people were inclined to forgive her for being stupid.

"Granny Grim-Eye used to send her with strawberries to sell to the rich man who owned nearly all the land in that part of the country. Now, this rich man fell in love with the Strawberry-Girl, but when he found that she was both stupid and silly he gave up all thought of marrying her. He was very fond of her, nevertheless, and bought all the berries she had for sale. But when she began to talk he would turn away with a sigh, for everything she said was stupid.

"It so happened one day that Granny Grim-Eye was too sick to pick the strawberries herself, as she always had done, and she was afraid to trust the Strawberry-Girl to pick them. But the rich man sent word that he was to have a company of friends to dinner and he must have some strawberries. There was nothing for Granny Grim-Eye to do but to send the Strawberry-Girl to the patch. Granny Grim-Eye called her up and cautioned her not to pick anything but good, ripe strawberries, and then sent her off to the patch.

"But on the way the Strawberry-Girl saw some red berries growing on bushes, and these she picked and put in the basket until it was full. 'These are just as red as ripe strawberries,' she said, 'and they will do just as well. Besides, they are a great deal easier to pick.'

"The way to the rich man's house led through a very thick wood, and while the Strawberry-Girl was going through this wood a little old man stepped from a hollow tree and stood in the path before her.

"'Aha!' says he, 'I find you alone at last. Where are you going, and what have you got?'

"'I am carrying some strawberries to your

master,' says the Strawberry-Girl, who imagined that the rich man was everybody's master.

"'My master!' cries the little old man; 'my master! But if he were my master, and I wanted to get rid of him, I'd not get in your path, for every berry in your basket is rank poison.'

"'Well, anyhow, they are red,' says the stupid Strawberry-Girl.

"'So they are,' says the little old man. 'But if you want to kill your master carry them to him.'

"'Oh, I don't want to kill him,' says the Strawberry-Girl. 'He pays too well.'

"'Once you belonged to me,' says the little old man. 'I tied you to a blackberry-bush with a fine silver chain, and left you there until I could attend to some business in the city. When I came back you were gone. I hunted for you high and low only to hear that you had been found by Granny Grim-Eye. What is the result? You have grown up beautiful and stupid. After all these years you don't know a strawberry from a dragon's-apple. If you had remained with me you would have grown to be the most beautiful as well as the wittiest woman in the world. You would have known everything that is hidden in nature — everything that has been stored between the lids of all the books.   It is a great pity!'

"'Yes,' says the stupid Strawberry-Girl, 'I expect it is; but what must I do with these berries? I haven't time to pick more?'

"'Well,' says the little old man, 'I'll make a bargain with you.   I'll fill your basket with the finest berries that were ever seen, and I'll make you the wittiest woman in the world if at the end of one year you will marry me.'

"The stupid Strawberry-Girl gave her promise, and then the little old man touched her on the forehead with his left thumb, pointed at a bright star with his right forefinger, and then went back to his hollow tree, warning the girl not to forget her promise.

"When she looked in the basket the red dragon's-apples had disappeared, and in their place she saw the finest strawberries that had ever been grown.   These she carried to the rich man, who was as much surprised at the size and lusciousness of the berries as his guests were at the extraordinary beauty of the young girl.   They praised her beauty to their host, who shook his head and said that beauty ceased to be beautiful when it was tied to stupidity. The guests, however, would not believe that so beautiful a creature could be stupid, and to satisfy them the rich man sent for the girl and engaged her in conversation. Her replies were so wise, so apt, and so witty, as to astound all the company, while the rich man was dumfounded with astonishment.

"After that, when the Strawberry-Girl came with berries for sale, the rich man always sent for her, and her wit and intelligence were so pleasing to him that he finally asked her to be his wife. But she remembered the bargain she had made with the little old man who had met her in the wood, and she told the rich man that she would have to take time to consider his proposal.

"She was very much worried. She fretted until she began to lose some of her beauty, and when Granny Grim-Eye saw this she began to ask questions, and it was not long before she found out all about the bargain the Strawberry-Girl had made with the little Old Man of the Wood.

"'Oho!' she cried. 'He is up to his old tricks, is he? Well, we shall see!'

"So she went to her chest and got the silver

chain with which the Strawberry-Girl had been fastened to the blackberry-bush, and wrapped and twined it in the shape of a star. This star she fixed on the Strawberry-Girl's forehead by means of a velvet band, and told her to wear it constantly.

"It happened that on the very day the year expired the Strawberry-Girl was walking through the wood. The little old man jumped from his hollow tree and ran forward to claim his bride. But when he saw the star shining on her forehead he gave a loud cry, threw his hands before his eyes, and turned and fled through the wood faster than any deer could have done. Nobody ever saw him again, and the Strawberry-Girl married the rich man and lived happily for many long years."

"I think that is a nice story," said Sweetest Susan.

"I'm glad you do," remarked Mr. Thimblefinger. "My mother knew all the facts in the case, and I've heard her tell it many a time. I may have left out some of the happenings, but these and many others you can supply for yourself."

XIV.

While Mr. Thimblefinger was telling the story of the Strawberry-Girl, Chickamy Crany Crow and Tickle-My-Toes had drawn near to listen. Chickamy Crany Crow stood near Mrs. Meadows, and seemed to be very much interested. When Mr. Thimblefinger had concluded, she would have gone away, but Mrs. Meadows detained her.

"No," said Mrs. Meadows, as Chickamy Crany Crow tried to pull her hand away; "you must stay right here and tell the children the story of the Witch of the Well."

"They know it already," said Chickamy Crany Crow, trying to hide behind Mrs. Meadows's chair.

"No, we don't," exclaimed Buster John. "We know the old rhyme about

"'Chickamy, Chickamy Crany Crow,
Went to the well to wash her toe,
And when she came back her chicken was gone.'

That's the rhyme we say in the game, but we never heard the story."

"I can't tell it to so many," said Chickamy Crany Crow.

"Well, tell it to me, then," replied Mrs. Meadows coaxingly. "The rest won't listen any more than they can help."

"Well," said Chickamy Crany Crow, "one time there was an old woman that lived near a well. For a long time nobody thought she was a witch, but after a while people began to have their suspicions. There was a quagmire in the road right in front of the old woman's house, and every traveler passing that way was sure to get mud on his feet. No matter whether he was riding horseback or in a buggy, it was all the same. He was sure to get his feet muddy. And the mud was so black, and thick, and heavy, that he was anxious to get it off as soon as possible.

"It happened, too, that every time a traveler crossed the quagmire, after getting the black, heavy mud on his feet, the old woman would be sitting in her door smoking a cob pipe.

"'Howdy, dearie!' she would say. 'Why,

you 're full of nasty mud! Go to the well yonder, dearie, and wash it off.'

" The traveler would leave his buggy and horse,
or his horse and saddle, or his bundle at the old
witch's door, and go to the well to wash his feet.
When he came back everything would be gone,
— witch, horse, buggy, saddle, or bundle. The
quagmire would be dried up, and the road itself
would seem to be a different road. Sometimes it
would be days and days before the traveler could
find his way to the place where he started.

" One day a traveler came along the road in a
fine carriage. With him he had a beautiful little
girl with long golden hair. She had eyes as blue
and as clear as the water in the spring when the
sunshine slants through, and her skin was as white
as milk. When the carriage had crossed the
quagmire, the traveler found that his feet were
covered with the black, heavy mud. He couldn't
imagine how it had happened. There was no
hole in the bottom of the carriage, the door was
shut tight, and there was no way for the mud to
get in. He said to the little girl: —

" ' Daughter, are your feet muddy? '

" ' Not a bit, father.'

"When the carriage crossed the quagmire, there sat the old woman in the door.

"'Howdy, dearie!' says she. 'And how did you get the nasty mud on your feet? Yonder is a well; leave your carriage here and go wash it off.'

"So the traveler kissed his daughter, for he was very fond of her, and went to the well to wash his feet. When he came back, daughter, carriage, and old woman had all disappeared. He wandered around like a crazy man for many days, and at last came to where my mother lived and told his story. This was n't the first time she had heard such a tale, and she concluded to see what the matter was. So she called me and gave me a black chicken and told me to go by the old woman's house and see what happened.

"I took the chicken, which was tied by the legs, and went along the road until I came to the quagmire. I tried to pick my way around it, but the black mud bubbled up and flew at my feet, and finally it became so thick and heavy I could scarcely walk. When I got across, there sat the old woman smoking her cob pipe and grinning.

"'Howdy, dearie!' says she.

" 'Howdy, granny !' says I.

" ' Leave your fat chicken here,' says she, ' and go to yonder well and wash your toe.'

" ' Thanky, granny ; that I will,' says I.

" So I went to the well, but when I came back my chicken was gone. And so was the old woman, and the quagmire. But I did n't get frightened. I went back to the well and began to sing, —

> " ' Chickamy, Chickamy Crany Crow,
> I went to the well to wash my toe,
> But when I came back my chicken was gone —
> What o'clock, old witch ? '

" I had n't been there long before the mud began to bubble up again, and out of it came the old witch. And then what seemed to be a thick mist cleared away, and there was the old witch's house, and inside I could see the beautiful little girl crying for her father. I intended to run home and tell what I had seen, but before I could move out of my tracks I heard the old woman coming to the well. In coming up out of the quagmire she had got mud on her feet. She had pulled off her shoes for comfort, and had been going about in her stocking-feet, and of course when she disappeared in the quagmire, and came up through it again, her stockings were full of mud; and so she came to the well to wash them.

"I didn't know whether to run or stay, but I stayed, and as soon as the old woman got in sight, I sat on the ground and began to rock my body backwards and forwards, crying, —

"'Oh, mercy me! Oh, what shall I do?
I can't get the black mud off of my shoe!'

"The old woman seemed to be very angry when she first saw me, but I pretended to pay no attention to her. I just rocked backwards and forwards, and cried that I couldn't get the black mud off of my shoe. The old woman sat down and pulled off her stockings, and began to wash them. When she had finished one, she threw it behind her on the grass to dry. Being wet and heavy it fell farther from her hand than she intended. It fell close to me, and I picked it up and stuffed it in my pocket."

"What for?" asked Buster John bluntly.

"Well, I hardly know," replied Chickamy Crany Crow, somewhat embarrassed at the suddenness of the question. "I wanted to get even with her for stealing my fat chicken. I hardly knew what I was doing, and I certainly didn't know how it would turn out. Well, I stuffed the old woman's wet stocking in my pocket, and kept on crying out that I didn't know how to get the black mud off of my shoe.

"'Do as I do,' said the old woman. Then I went and sat on the grass in front of her, and washed the mud from my shoe.

"For the first time I saw what a horrible-looking creature the old woman was. Her eyes were sunk in her head, her nose was hooked over her mouth, and she had two long upper teeth that hung lower than her under lip. I says to myself, 'Well, old lady, if you are not a witch, there never was one.' She washed her stocking, mumbling and chewing, and when she had finished she threw it behind her, and sat hugging her knees, and glaring at me in a way that made my flesh crawl.

"'What is your name?' says she.

"'Chickamy Crany Crow,' says I.

"'What are you doing here?' says she.

"Says I, 'I went to the well to wash my toe, but when I came back my chicken was gone.'

"Then the old woman began to laugh like a cackling hen, and she laughed so loud and laughed so long that it scared me. I got up and pretended to be going home, but when I had gone a little way I hid behind a big tree, and watched the old woman's antics. She kept on laughing for some time, and then she reached out for her stockings. She found the only one she had left, and put it on. Then she reached around for the other, but failed to find it, because I had it in my pocket. This seemed to puzzle her. She stood up and looked all around for her missing stocking, but it was n't there. Then she sat down again, pulled off the stocking she had on, and put it on the other foot.

"But she still lacked a stocking. This seemed to puzzle the old witch worse than ever. Once more she pulled off the stocking and put it on the other foot, and appeared to be very much astonished because one foot was still bare."

"She could n't 'a' had much sense!" exclaimed Drusilla.

"Not about stockings and things like that," said Chickamy Crany Crow. "Well, she sat there, pulling the stocking from one foot and putting it on the other, until she seemed to forget about everything else. I watched her until I got tired, and then I thought I would take her missing stocking and throw it in the quagmire.

"The moment I did this, the quagmire began to bubble, and hiss, and roll, and toss and tumble about, and soon it disappeared altogether. A little fog arose when the quagmire sank out of sight, and when this cleared away, there stood the carriage that had brought the beautiful little girl with the golden hair, and the little girl herself was sitting in it, ready to go to her father. But this wasn't all. All around, there were numbers of horses and buggies, and all sorts of bundles and money-purses, and everything that travelers carry along with them.

"Well, I got in the carriage with the beautiful little girl, clucked to the horses, and drove to my mother's house. All the horses with saddles, and all the horses hitched to buggies, followed along after us, and there was great rejoicing among the people as we went by."

"What became of the old witch?" asked Buster John.

"She stayed there, trying to make one stocking do for two feet, until the well dried up, and after that I don't know what became of her."

"You ought to have been a young man," said Sweetest Susan, who had been reading fairy stories, "so that you could have married the beautiful girl with golden hair, after rescuing her. Besides, your name would have been in the books."

"Oh," answered Chickamy Crany Crow, smiling for the first time, "there are plenty of names in the books that you never hear of; but now, wherever little children get together to play games, you will hear them saying the rhyme that tells a part of my story, —

> "'Chickamy, Chickamy Crany Crow,
> Went to the well to wash her toe,
> But when she got back her chicken was gone.'"

XV.

THE BEWITCHED HUNTSMAN.

" THERE used to be a great many more witches than there are now," remarked Mr. Thimble-finger. " I reckon it 's because folks have more business of their own to attend to; or, it may be a change in the climate. I hear old people say that the winters are colder now than they used to be, and the summers hotter. Maybe that has something to do with it. Anyhow, something has happened to thin the witches out."

" Yes," said Mr. Rabbit; " I 've noticed that they are scarcer than they used to be, but I never inquired into the whys and wherefores. They never bothered me, and I never bothered them."

" Well, when I first came here," said Mr. Thim-blefinger, " I noticed Jimmy Jay-Bird bringing sand and mortar every Friday, and it occurred to me that he was preparing to lay the foundations of a witch's house in this country. So I says to myself, says I, ' I 'll keep an eye on Jimmy, and see

where he gets in and out; for, surely, he does n't
come by way of the spring.' But Jimmy Jay-Bird
was pretty slick, and it was some time before I
found out where he came down and went out. By
some means or other, he had discovered the big
hollow poplar on the spring branch, and he was
coming and going that way."

"I know where it is," said Buster John.

"Yes," replied Mr. Thimblefinger. "It is the
oldest and the biggest tree in the whole country
next door. But as soon as I found that Jimmy
Jay-Bird was using it as a passageway, I drove a
peg in the hole and put an end to his schemes,
whatever they may have been. I don't know
where he carries his sand and mortar now, and
I don't care.

"But I did n't start out to tell anything about
Jimmy Jay-Bird," continued Mr. Thimblefinger,
after pausing a moment. "I was thinking about
the way a witch was caught by a boy no bigger
and not much older than our young friend here."

"Tell us about it, please!" cried Buster John
enthusiastically.

"Well," said Mr. Thimblefinger, "it's not
much of a story. You can't take a handful of

facts and make a story of them unless you know
how to fling them together. The best I can do
is to tell it just as it happened as near as I can
remember.

"When I was a little bit of a fellow — now
don't laugh!" cried Mr. Thimblefinger, seeing
Mr. Rabbit wink at Mrs. Meadows, — "I mean
when I was in my teens. Well, when I was
younger than I am now, an old witch lived not
far from our house. Her eyes were red around
the rims, and her eyeballs looked as if they had
been boiled. Everybody called her Peggy Pig-
Eye, and she answered to that name about as well
as she did to any other. Near her house there
lived a man who had a wife and a son. He was
a tolerably well-to-do man, and all the neighbors
thought very well of him. But he used to go to
town every sale-day, and at night he would come
home feeling very gay. I don't know what there
was in town to make him feel so gay, but I know
that he used to come by our house singing at the
top of his voice and cutting up all sorts of shines.

"Well, one night when he was going back
home whooping and yelling, he saw something
dark in the road before him, and he rode his

horse at it full tilt. The horse seemed to have little taste for such sport, for he snorted and wanted to shy around the dark object. But the man clapped spurs to the horse and drove him right at it. The black thing ran, and the man spurred his horse after it. It ran down the road, then across an old field and back into the road again, the man pursuing it as hard as he could make his horse go. Finally it ran into Peggy Pig-Eye's yard and under her house, and the man went clattering after it. Just as he pulled his horse up (to keep the animal from running broadside into the house) the door opened, and Peggy Pig-Eye put her head out.

"'Oh, it's you, is it?' she cried. 'And you are after me, are you? Very well!' With that she clapped the door to, and the man rode on home, not feeling as lively as he had felt.

"Now, it happened that this man was a great hunter. He had a pack of fine dogs, and he was very fond of them. He hunted deer with them by day, and raccoons and 'possums by night. The first time he went hunting after riding into Peggy Pig-Eye's yard was at night. He didn't go very far from his house before his dogs struck

a warm trail and went scurrying towards the big
swamp at a great rate. A negro, who went along
to carry the light and cut the tree down, shook
his head and declared the dogs were not barking
to suit him. He said there was more whine than
growl to the noise they were making.

"Anyhow, the dogs went scurrying to the big
swamp, and the man and the negro followed as
fast as they could. The dogs treed right at the
edge of the swamp, and when the man and the
negro got there, they were barking up a big poplar. The negro held his torch behind him so as
to 'shine' in the raccoon's eyes, — if it was a
raccoon, — but he could see nothing.

"'Cut the tree down,' said the man.

The negro shook his head, but he whacked
away at the poplar with his axe, and cut it so
that it would fall away from the swamp. The
tree fell with a tremendous crash, and the dogs
rushed into the top limbs, followed by the man
and the negro. But before they could wink
their eyes, something tall and white walked out,
and cried : —

"'*You are always after me!*'

"The negro threw down the torch and the axe,

and ran home as fast as he could. The dogs tried hard to catch the white thing, whatever it was, but as soon as they got near enough to bite it, they tucked their tails between their legs and ran howling back to their master.

" This happened every time the man went out to hunt raccoons and 'possums. The dogs would strike a warm trail not far from the house, run to the edge of the swamp, and bay up a tree, and then when the tree was cut down, something tall and white would walk from the top limbs, and cry out:

" '*You are always after me!*'

" The man thought it was very queer, but he wasn't frightened. He said to himself that if he couldn't catch raccoons and 'possums, maybe he could catch a fox. So he called up his dogs one morning just about day, mounted his horse, and started out to catch a fox. Before they had gone a hundred yards from the house, the dogs found a warm trail and began to follow it in lively style. The man spurred his horse after them and harked them on. They ran around in a wide circle, and presently something white flitted by the man, with the dogs after it in full cry. As it went by it screamed out : —

" '*You are always after me!* '

" Then it disappeared, and after a while the dogs came back, panting as hard as if they had run forty miles. The man went back home and sat by the fire and studied about it, and the more he studied the worse he was troubled. He sat so long without saying anything that his little boy asked him what the matter was, but the man shook his head, and said there were some things that children ought not to know. The boy was fourteen years old, and very small for his age, but he had plenty of sense, and was very brave. He told his mother that his father was in some deep trouble, and begged her to find out what it was, and tell him about it.

" So the little boy's mother set herself to work to find out what was troubling her husband. She pressed him so hard with questions that he finally told her about his strange adventures while out hunting. The wife was so frightened that she begged her husband not to go hunting any more, but to give up his dogs and attend to business that was not so dangerous.

" The man promised that he would hunt no more raccoons or 'possums or foxes, but he said

he needed his dogs to hunt deer.   The woman
told her son all that her husband had said to
her, and after that the little boy made it a habit
to go off in the woods and sit at the foot of a big
chestnut-tree, and wonder what it was that ran
before his father's dogs.

"Matters went on this way until finally one
day the man said he would go out and catch a
deer.   He called his dogs, especially Old Top, the
oldest one of all.   Top was a big hound, and hunted
nothing else but deer, and he was never known
to fail to run down and catch the deer he got after.
Old Top went along when he was called, but it
was very plain to the little boy, who was watching,
that he didn't go willingly.   Anyhow, Old Top
went, though he looked back at the little boy and
wagged his tail knowingly more than once.

"Before the hunter got out of hearing, the
dogs struck a trail and pursued it in the direction of the big woods beyond the creek.   For
a long time the little boy listened to the dogs running.   Sometimes they seemed to come nearer,
and then they would go farther, and finally the
sound of their trailing died away altogether.

"After waiting and listening for some time,

the little boy went into the woods and sat at the foot of the chestnut-tree. While he was sitting there thinking, and watching the big black ants chase each other up and down the tree, he heard the bushes shake, and suddenly a little old man appeared before him.

"'Heyday!' said the little old man. 'You are too young to be thinking. Leave thoughts for old people; you should be at play.'

"'But sometimes,' replied the little boy, 'children have to think, too. It does n't make my headache to think.'

"'I see, I see!' exclaimed the little old man; 'your name is Three Wits. Three Wits, how are you? I hope you are well. You ought to have come here a little sooner. There is a famous hunt going on in these woods. It passed here awhile ago — a fool on a frightened horse and seven crazy dogs galloping after Satan's sister. Oh, it is jolly! Stay where you are, Three Wits. This famous hunt will pass this way again directly, and you will have a plain view of it.'

"After a while the little boy heard the dogs coming, and presently he saw the strangest sight his eyes had ever beheld. Going through the

woods as swift as the wind, he saw a great white
Stag. On the back of the Stag, and holding to
its antlers, was an old woman. She was grinning
horribly, and her gray hair was streaming out behind her like a ragged banner. The Stag, bear-
ing the old woman, rushed through the woods
and disappeared. Then came the dogs in full
cry, and after the dogs came the little boy's
father, spurring his horse and yelling in the excitement of the chase.

"'What do you think of it, Three Wits?'
asked the little old man, laughing.

"'I don't like it,' replied the boy. 'That man
is my father.'

"'Your father!' cried the little old man.
'Oho! That alters the case. Well, well! Let's
see — let's see!'

"The little old man took from the wallet he
had on his back a thick book with a red cover.
Then he sat at the foot of the chestnut-tree and
turned the well-thumbed leaves until he found the
place he was hunting for. He closed the book,
but kept his forefinger between the leaves, and
took the little boy's hand in his.

XVI.

THE THREE IVORY BOBBINS.

"The little old man took the boy's hand in his, but before he could say anything, a rustling was heard in the bushes. Presently, Old Top, the deerhound, made his appearance. He went up to the boy, smelt of him, wagged his tail as a sign of satisfaction, and then curled up in the leaves as if to take a nap. But he didn't go to sleep. Every once in awhile, Old Top raised his head and listened wistfully to the running dogs that could be heard in the distance.

"'A very sensible dog!' exclaimed the little old man. 'He knows something is wrong.'

"'What is it?' asked the boy.

"'Well, Three Wits,' said the little old man, 'I'll tell you. The man, the horse, and the dogs, are under a spell. They are bewitched, and they will continue to be bewitched until doomsday, unless the spell is broken. They will go round and round on the trail until they exhaust them-

selves, and then they will gradually grow thinner
and thinner until they disappear; and then nothing will be heard but the barking of the dogs,
and the sound of that will grow fainter and
fainter, until no human ear can hear it.   Now,
the question is, Three Wits, do you wish the spell
broken ? '

"'I do,' replied the boy, 'for my mother's
sake.'

"'Now that is well spoken,' said the old man,
rising and laying his hand gently on the boy's
head.   'For, behold, Three Wits, what is written
in the book.'

"The old man opened the red volume and read
as follows, pointing to each word with his finger : —

"'Whoever shall, for the sake of his mother,
earnestly desire to break the spells worked by
Paggia Paggiola, the Hunting-Witch, is in a way
to have his desire fulfilled.   For this is the indis-
pensable condition.   Moreover, he who hopes to
succeed must have the innocence of youth and
the courage of manhood.   On his left arm there
should grow a mole, and in this mole are three
white hairs.'

" 'I have the mole,' said the boy, opening his vest.

"Sure enough, there was the mole, and on the mole were growing three long white hairs as fine as silk. With a pair of silver tweezers that he found in his wallet, the little old man pulled the long white hairs from the mole. One by one he pulled them. One by one he ran them through his fingers, and one by one they seemed to grow longer and stronger, each time they were pulled through the little old man's swift-moving fingers.

"Then, searching in his wallet, he found three ivory bobbins; and on these he wound the long, strong, and silken hairs. He wound and wound, and as he wound he sang : —

> " 'Now on this bobbin I wind a hair,
> White, and silken, and long ;
> I wind it slow, I wind it fair,
> Glossy, and white, and strong.

> " 'I wind it here in shade and sun,
> For one, one, one are three —
> Three and no more where the stag shall run,
> Close by the chestnut-tree.

> " 'And one shall catch, and two shall hold,
> And three shall clamp and kill ;

Just say to your hand, Be steady and bold ;
And say to your heart, I will.'

" The boy was surprised to see, as the old man
sang and wound, that the white hairs spun out
into silver wires hundreds of feet long, and
stronger than steel.

" ' Take these, Three Wits,' said the old man,
after he had finished winding the bobbins. ' Take
these, and when the hunt runs this way again,
fling one at the Stag, and one at the dogs, and
one at the horse the huntsman rides. You must
fling them quickly, one after the other. It is
easy enough to miss the Stag, but you must not
fail to catch the dogs. You may fail on the Stag
and horse, but you must not fail on the dogs.
Be strong. Brace yourself for three quick and
hard throws.'

" Then they stood there listening ; and presently Old Top, the deerhound, raised his head and
whistled through his nose, the whistle ending in
a whine.

" ' They are coming now, Three Wits !' exclaimed the little old man. ' Get ready ! Throw
quick and hard ! Don't be afraid !'

" In the distance, the baying of the dogs could

be heard, and Old Top rose and shook himself
and growled. In another moment the Stag,
ridden by the grinning old woman, flitted past ;
but, quick as a flash, Three Wits threw the first
bobbin, and he threw it so hard that it made a
zooning sound in the air. The Stag made one
tremendous bound and disappeared. The dogs
came next, and Three Wits threw the second bobbin. It zooned through the air, and the silver
wire unwound with a twanging sound, and fell
full upon the panting and baying pack. It fell
upon them, and wound itself about them, and
smothered their cries, and held them fast in its
glistening meshes.

"Then came the rushing horse and its furious
rider. Three Wits threw the third bobbin, but the
horse shied at the motion of the boy's hand, and
flew through the woods in the direction taken by
the Stag. When Three Wits saw both the Stag
and the horse escape, he fell upon the ground
and began to weep.

"' Hity-tity !' exclaimed the little old man,
coming from behind the tree where he had
concealed himself. 'What 's this? Why, I was
about to cry "Bravo !" and here I find you pre

tending to be a baby. Get up. If I am not
mistaken you have accomplished even more than
I expected you would. Let's see.'

" He lifted Three Wits to his feet, and then the
two went to where the hunt had passed. At one
point the dogs were entangled in the silver wire,
and were unable to free themselves. A little
farther in, they found a thick wisp of gray hair
which the wire had cut from the head of the
grinning old woman who rode the Stag. The
little old man clapped his hands with delight and
cut some joyful capers, for he was very nimble.

" ' Good !' he exclaimed. ' Another half inch
and you would have cut off her head instead
of her hair ! But where is the bobbin ? I don't
see the bobbin ! We must have the bobbin !'

" Three Wits hunted, but he could find no
bobbin. Then he caught hold of the wire, and
found that it led into the woods the way the Stag
had gone. He caught hold of it and followed it
along, calling to the little old man. They followed the silver wire far into the woods, and
finally they came to the end of it, and there was
the Stag, strangled and dead. The weight of the
bobbin had carried the wire around his body

and around his neck, and the bobbin itself had caught in the fork of one of his antlers.

"The little old man seemed to be very happy. He patted Three Wits on the shoulder, and declared that he was a good boy, a fine boy. 'But there is more to be done,' said the little old man, — 'a great deal more. And you will have to go alone. I can help you, but I can't be with you.'

"Then he found the ivory bobbins, rewound the silver wire, which seemed to spin out still longer, and gave them to Three Wits. 'Take these,' he said, 'and go to the witch's house.'

"'Do you mean Peggy Pig-Eye's house?' asked Three Wits.

"'Why, of course,' replied the little old man. 'Her right name, as you saw by the book, is Paggia Paggiola, but people call her Peggy Pig-Eye for short. Go to her house, throw one of the bobbins over the roof, and then throw one around each end. Throw quick and hard, and, as you throw, cry out, —

> "'Bibbity bobbity bobbin,
> Go hibbity hob hobnobbin.'

"'But wait!' cried the little old man. 'You

may need these dogs.' He took a wisp of the witch's hair, and whipped them back to life. And maybe you 'll need a horse to ride. So he went into the woods where the Stag lay dead, and whipped him to his feet with the witch's hair.

"'This is your horse,' he said to Three Wits. But the boy was afraid to mount the Stag. 'Be bold!' cried the little old man; 'all depends on that! Give me your foot. There you are! Loop the silver wire over his horns, and touch him with the bobbin the way you want him to go. He'll carry you safely. Good-by! Be bold!'

"Following the little old man's directions, Three Wits was soon cantering down the road on the Stag's back. The dogs seemed to take everything for granted, and followed along after the Stag as readily as if he had been their master's horse. But travelers who chanced to be going along the road went into the wood when they saw a boy riding a big Stag. They were not used to such a queer sight.

"The spirits of Three Wits rose as he went along. Everything had turned out so happily, and the Stag moved along so gracefully and easily that Three Wits felt quite like a hero.

"He went ambling along the road, the people staring at him, until he came to the witch's house. Everything was quiet there. The windows and doors were closed, and the only sign of life about the place was a big black cat that sat on the water-shelf. Three Wits rode the Stag around the house three times. Then over the roof he threw a bobbin. To the right he threw another, and to the left another. The silver wire seemed to whirl until it became a tangle of wire all over the house. The big black cat made an attempt to escape, but it was caught in the wire as a fly is caught in a spider's web, and it hung helpless by the water-shelf.

"And then a very wonderful thing happened. The silver wire seemed to become so heavy that the roof of the house couldn't bear its weight. The cabin swayed, and finally the roof fell in with a crash. Out of the dust and wreck walked the father of Three Wits, leading his horse, and, following him, came a dozen or more elegantly dressed gentlemen whom Three Wits had never seen before. They shook hands with the boy and thanked him for coming to their rescue, and each gave him a large sum of gold, so that when they started on their way home, Three Wits found that he was very rich. As for the father, he seized Three Wits in his arms and embraced him again and again, and declared that even a king might be proud to have such a brave son.

"While they were talking, the little old man came out of the wood. He went straight to Three Wits, placed his hand on the boy's head, and seemed to be blessing him. Then he lifted Three Wits from the Stag's back, mounted in his place, waved his hand twice, and, in a twinkling, had disappeared in the wood. That was the end of the witch, and this is the end of the story."

"Well, I think it is a very good story," said Buster John.

"I think so, too," remarked Sweetest Susan; "but I'm sorry there was no little girl in it."

XVII.

"KEEN-POINT," "COB-HANDLE," AND "BUTCH."

"The three bobbins," said Mrs. Meadows, "remind me of a circumstance —"

"Is a circumstance a story?" interrupted Sweetest Susan.

"Oh, you must n't mind my country talk," replied Mrs. Meadows, laughing. "It was a trick of my tongue. I did n't want to say 'story' because you might be disappointed. But I reckon I may as well call it a story. Well, as I was saying, the three bobbins remind me of a story that was partly about a little girl."

"I know it must be a nice story," cried Sweetest Susan enthusiastically.

But Mrs. Meadows shook her head. "From all I can hear," she said, "matters and things in general are a great deal nicer in books than they are outside of books. Folks are folks, anyway you can fix them, I don't care what the books say. But I 'll not deny that in my day and time

I have seen folks mighty near as nice and as pretty as those you read about in the books, and one of these was the little girl I am going to tell you about.

"Once upon a time, in the country where I then lived, — and I've lived in a good many countries, for wherever you find mountains, hills, and rivers, there you'll find the Meadows family, — there was a little girl who was both beautiful and good. She was not as good nor as beautiful as those you read about in the books, but she was good enough for the people who knew her. For a wonder she did n't have long golden hair. Her hair was black, and curled about her head in the loveliest way; and her eyes were large and brown, and her skin creamy white, with just the shadow of rose color in her face. Her parents were rich and proud, but they were prouder of their little girl than they were of their money, as well they might be, seeing that she was the smartest and most beautiful child to be found in all the country round."

"Were there no princes and castles in that country?" inquired Sweetest Susan.

"Oh, dear, no!" replied Mrs. Meadows.

"The folks were just plain, common, every-day people. Those that were fortunate enough to be honest and contented were much better off than any princes you ever heard of; and a hut where happiness lives is a much finer place than the finest castle.

"Well, as I was telling you, the parents of this little girl with black curly hair were very proud of her. They watched over her very carefully, and neglected nothing that would make her happy and contented. Some little girls that I have known would have been spoiled by so much kindness and attention, but this little girl with the black curly hair wasn't spoiled at all. She was as good as she was beautiful.

"One day, when this little girl was walking in the flower garden, she heard the gardener talking to his wife through the iron fence. The woman's voice was so pleasant and her laugh so cheerful that the little girl ran to the fence and peeped through to see who it was. The gardener's wife saw her, and at once began to pet her and make much of her. The little girl wanted the woman to come into the garden, and seemed to be so much in earnest about it that the woman promised she would come and be the child's nurse some day.

"No sooner had the gardener's wife gone about her business than the little girl ran and told her mother that she must have a nurse. At first her mother paid little attention to her, thinking that it was the passing whim of a child, but the little girl insisted, until finally her mother said: —

"'Who shall be your nurse? You know, my dear, that you can't have everybody and anybody?'

"'Ask the gardener,' the little girl replied. 'He knows.'

"'And how does he know?' the mother asked.

"'I saw him talking with her,' the little girl replied.

"So, after a time, the gardener was called, and then it was found that his wife was the person the little girl had selected to be her nurse. The father and mother hesitated for some time before they would consent to send for the woman, but finally she came, and they were so much struck by her pleasant manners and cheerful disposition that they were quite willing to employ her.

"For a long time after that the little girl and her nurse were never separated except when the nurse

would go home to see her husband and her son,
who was a handsome boy about fourteen years old.
The little girl used to grieve so when her nurse
left her that on one occasion, when the woman was
going home for only an hour or so, she carried
the child with her. There the little girl saw the
handsome son of her nurse, and they were both
very much pleased with each other. In the little
time she stayed, the boy showed her a hundred
new games, and told her a great many stories she
had never heard before."

"How old was the little girl?" Mr. Thimblefinger inquired.

"Between seven and eight," replied Mrs.
Meadows "Just old enough to be cute. Well,
in the little time they were together the boy and
girl grew to be very fond of each other. The
boy thought she was the daintiest and prettiest
creature he had ever seen, and the little girl
thought the boy was all that a boy should be.

"Of course, when the little girl went back
home again she talked of nothing else but the
boy who had proved to be such a wonderful playmate. This set the child's mother to thinking,
and she made up her mind that it wouldn't do

for these children to see so much of each other. So she sent for the nurse and told her very kindly that she did n't think it would be prudent to carry the little girl to her house any more.

" The nurse agreed with the little girl's mother, but somehow she did n't relish the idea that her brave and handsome son was n't good enough to play with anybody's daughter. She thought the matter over for several days, and finally decided that it would be better to give up her place as nurse. She was very fond of the little girl, but she was still fonder of her boy. So she ceased to be the child's nurse, and went to her own home.

"The little girl grieved day and night for her kind nurse. Nothing would console her. Her mother bought her a little pony, but she would n't ride it; wonderful dolls, but she would n't look at them; the finest cakes and candies, but she would n't eat them; the most beautiful dresses, but she would n't wear them. Matters went on in this way for I don't know how long, until, finally, one day the little girl's mother concluded to send for the nurse.

" Now it happened that on that particular day the little girl had made up her mind to go after her nurse. One day in each week, the gardener would open the big gates of the park in order to trundle away the trash and weeds that he had raked up. The little girl watched him open the gate, and then, when the gardener went for his wheelbarrow, she slipped out at the gate and went running across the fields.

" For a time the little girl was perfectly happy. She gave herself up to the pleasure of being alone, of being able to do as she chose, with no one to tell her not to do this or do that, or to say ' come here,' or ' go yonder.' So she went running across the fields, looking at the birds, and trying to catch butterflies, and singing to herself some of the beautiful songs that her nurse's son had taught her.

" Now it happened that when she ran out of the garden gate, in her haste to keep out of sight of the gardener, she went away from her nurse's house instead of going towards it. She had been kept so closely at home that she had no idea of the great world beyond the garden gate. She thought that all she had to do to get to her dear nurse's house was to go out at the gate and keep on going until she came to the place where there were two big trees, with a swing between them, and a little white house on the other side.

"So she went on her way, singing and skipping. When she grew tired she sat down to rest. When she grew thirsty she drank of the clear, cold water that ran through the fields. When she became hungry, she ate the berries that grew along the way. She was perfectly satisfied that she would soon come to her nurse's house. But the sun does n't stop for grown people, much less for children, and the little girl soon found that night was coming on. The only thought she had was that her nurse's house had been moved farther away, and that by going straight ahead she would find it after a while.

"So she trudged along. When the sun was nearly down she saw an old man sitting in the shade of a tree. The little girl went straight towards him, made him a curtsey, as she had been taught to do, and said : —

"' Please, sir, where is my nurse's house?'

"The old man raised his head and glanced all around. 'I see no nurse's house,' he replied.

"Then, after a little while the old man said: 'My dear, give me a drink of water.'

"The little girl looked all around. 'I see no water,' she replied.

"'Well said, well said!' exclaimed the old man. 'You are very bright and very beautiful, therefore I'll give you some advice. There is a spring by yonder tree, but you must not drink the water. There is a pomegranate-tree growing by the spring, but you must eat none of the fruit.'

"Having said this, the old man slung his wallet over his back and went on his way. The little girl went to the spring and looked at the water. Then she looked at the beautiful red fruit growing on the pomegranate-tree. She was very thirsty, very hungry, and very tired. She thought to herself that the old man was very mean and stingy. 'He's afraid I'll muddy the water,' she said, 'and he wants all the pomegranates for himself.'

"Then she drank from the spring, and the water was very sweet and cool. She ate the fruit of the pomegranate-tree, and it was delicious. Then being tired, she stretched herself out on the grass and was soon sound asleep.

"Now it so happened," continued Mrs. Meadows, pretending to examine the stitches in

Sweetest Susan's frock "that the spring and the pomegranate-tree were under a spell. They belonged to an old Conjurer who lived in a cave close by. In this cave he had a large bowl of water on a shelf, and near it, growing in a box, was a little pomegranate-bush. Whenever anybody drank from the spring, the water in the bowl would shake and tremble and become muddy; and whenever a pomegranate was pulled from the big bush by the spring, the little bush in the Conjurer's cave would bend and wave its limbs as if a gale were blowing.

"All this occurred when the little girl drank from the spring and pulled and ate one of the pomegranates; and by the time she was sound asleep, the Conjurer had come out of his cave and discovered her. He waited a little while, and then took the child and carried her to his cave, and it was many a long day before anybody, except the Conjurer himself, saw her again."

At this point Mrs. Meadows paused.

XVIII.

THE pause was occasioned by Mr. Rabbit. He had fallen into a doze while Mrs. Meadows was telling her story, and just as she came to the point where the Conjurer had lifted the little girl in his arms and carried her into his cave, Mr. Rabbit had dreamed that he was falling. His chair was tilted back a little, and he made such a mighty effort to keep himself from falling in his dream that he lost his balance and went over sure enough.

"I declare!" he exclaimed. "I ought to be ashamed of myself to be falling heels over head this way without any reason in the world, and right before company too. Wasn't there something in your story about falling?"

"Not a word!" replied Mrs. Meadows firmly.

"Well, well, well!" exclaimed Mr. Rabbit. "I'll try and keep my eyes open hereafter."

The children tried their best to keep from

laughing at Mr. Rabbit's predicament, but Drusilla was finally compelled to give way to her desire, and then they all joined in, even Mr. Rabbit smiling somewhat grimly.

"Let me see," said Mrs. Meadows, after a while; "the last we heard of the little girl I was telling you about, the Conjurer had carried her into his cave?"

"Yes," answered Sweetest Susan; "and now I want to know what became of her."

"Well," said Mrs. Meadows, "the shortest way to tell you that is the best way. It happened that on the very day the little girl ran away to visit her nurse, the nurse had concluded to visit the little girl. So she put on her best things and went to the little girl's home. When the woman came to the garden she saw the gate open, and presently her husband, the gardener, came out trundling a load of weeds and trash in his wheelbarrow. She asked about the little girl.

"'She was playing under the trees yonder awhile ago,' said the man. 'I haven't seen her since.'

"'The woman went into the garden and searched

among the trees and arbors, but no little girl could she find.

"'Having come so far,' she said to herself, 'I'll not go back without seeing the precious little creature.' So she went towards the house, searching for the child. She inquired of every servant she met where the little girl was, and finally went into the house searching for her. At last she came to the room where sat her former mistress. But the child was not there.

"In a very short while there was a tremendous uproar in the place. The maid servants and the men servants went running about through the house, through the yard, and through the garden, calling the little girl. They hunted in every hole and corner, and in every nook and cranny, but the child was not to be found.

"The kind-hearted nurse wept almost as bitterly as the mother. 'Oh, if I had been here,' she cried, 'this would never have happened.'

"The little girl's father came in just in time to hear this, and he immediately suspected that the nurse had stolen his daughter and would pretend to find her again in the hope of securing a reward. He said nothing of his suspicions, but he determined to have the nurse closely watched.

"He was so firmly convinced that his suspicion was correct that he treated his daughter's disappearance somewhat lightly, and this helped to console the mother. When it became certain that the little girl was not to be found in the house or on the place, her father called one of his trusty clerks (for he was a rich and powerful merchant), and told him to disguise himself as a peddler, go to the nurse's house, and there discover, if possible, where the nurse had bestowed the child.

"The clerk did as he was directed, but when he arrived at the nurse's house, disguised as a peddler, he was surprised to find as much grief under that humble roof as there was at his master's house. He knocked at the door and inquired the cause of the trouble, hoping to discover that the display of grief was a mere sham. But he soon saw it was genuine. Both the woman and her handsome son were weeping bitterly over the disappearance of the little girl.

"'May I get a bite to eat?' asked the peddler.

"'That you may!' exclaimed the woman, 'for

we shall need nothing ourselves, until we hear
.some news of that precious child.' Then she
told the peddler about the strange disappearance
of the little girl she used to nurse, and the peddler, in order to carry out his purpose, asked a
great many questions. When he was told that
the parents of the little girl were very rich he
laughed, and said that if they had plenty of
money they could get along very well without a
little girl, but this made the woman and her son
so angry that they were on the point of showing
the peddler the door. They were ready to dis-
miss him with many hard words, when they heard
some one calling.

"The son went into the yard, and found that
an old man had fallen not far from their gate and
was unable to rise. The woman went to help her
son bring the old man in, and while they were
gone the peddler took his leave without so much
as saying good-by.

"With a good deal of trouble the old man
was brought into the house, and made comfortable, but no sooner had he been placed upon the
woman's bed than he leaped to his feet and stood
on the floor, laughing.

"'I have fallen at a dozen doors to-day,' he cried, 'and this is the first that has been opened to me.'

"'Well,' replied the woman, 'if we had known you were playing pranks on us I don't think this door would have opened to you. We are having too much trouble ourselves to pester with other people's troubles.'

"Then she went on to tell of the disappearance of the little girl she used to nurse. The old man tried to get in a word of consolation, now and then, but the woman talked too fast for that. But presently she had told about all she had to tell.

"'See how it turns out!' cried the old man. 'How can it be accident that brings to your door the only person in the world that can give you any tidings of the little girl? I saw a child to-day some miles from here who asked me to show her her nurse's house.'

"'Bless her dear little heart!' exclaimed the woman.

"'But she was in great danger,' said the old man. 'She was just about to enter the domain of Rimrak.'

"'Ah, why did n't you bring her away with you?' cried the woman.

"'It is not permitted,' replied the old man. 'I did what I could. I warned her not to drink of the waters of the spring nor to eat of the pomegranate-seed. I could do no more.'

"'Oh, what will become of the dear child?' exclaimed the woman, wringing her hands.

"'If she drinks of the waters of the spring,' responded the old man, 'or eats of the pomegranate-seed, she will fall into a deep sleep. Then will come Rimrak, the Conjurer, and convey her to his cave, and there she will be held captive until she forgets she is a captive, or until she has been rescued by some bold youth who loves her well enough to remember the color of her eyes.'

"'I remember! I remember!' cried the woman's handsome son.

"'Be not too sure,' replied the old man. 'Sit down and think it over.'

"'No need for that,' said the boy. 'Her eyes once seen can never be forgotten.'

"'Oho!' exclaimed the old man. 'Then perhaps you can tell me the color of the little girl's eyes?'

"'Certainly,' said the boy. 'They are brown when she lifts them to your face and dark when she looks away from you.'

"The old man nodded his head with a greater display of good humor than he had yet shown.

"'Ah, you think so,' said the old man, warningly; 'you think you know, but be not too sure.'

"'Why, I can see her now!' exclaimed the boy.

"'Where?' cried his mother; 'oh, where?'

"The boy fell back in his seat and covered his face with his hands.

"'He was speaking of his memory,' said the old man. 'If he can trust it, well and good.'

"You should have brought the child home with you,' said the matter-of-fact woman.

"'It was not in my power,' replied the old man. 'She had gone too far. She had already entered the domain of Rimrak, the Conjurer. All that I could do I did. I warned her not to drink of the waters of the spring. I warned her not to eat of the seed of the pomegranate. But now that I am here, let us see what can be done.'

"He went to his wallet, which he had placed on the table, opened it and took from it three knives. One was a clasp-knife with a long, slim blade, the next was a common case-knife, and the third was a big butcher's-knife. The case-knife had once had a horn or wooden handle, but this had dropped off, and the iron that held the knife in place had been run into a corncob. The old man took these knives from his wallet, one by one, and placed them on the table.

"'Now listen to me,' he said to the boy. 'All will go well with you if you are bold, and if you really remember the color of the little girl's eyes. Here are your arms. This,' taking up the clasp-knife, 'is Keen-Point. This,' taking up the case-knife, 'is Cob-Handle. And this is Butch. Remember their names, — Keen-Point, Cob-Handle, and Butch. Keen-Point is to show you the way, Cob-Handle is to warn you of danger, and Butch is to protect you. But they will all fail you — they will all go wrong — if you do not remember the color of the little girl's eyes.'

"The boy took Keen-Point, Cob-Handle, and Butch, and stowed them away in a wallet, in which his mother placed a supply of food. Then he set out on his journey, with a light heart. He was not afraid, for he knew that he loved the little girl well enough to remember the color of her eyes. He went on his way till he came to the open fields where no one lived. He had been there many a time before, but now it seemed to him that he had never seen so many paths and by-ways. They led in all directions and crossed each other almost at every turn.

" He stopped and looked all around, and then he took Keen-Point from his wallet, and said: —

" ' Keen-Point can, Keen-Point may,
Point keen and true, and show me the way.'

" As soon as he said this, the knife tumbled from his hand and fell to the ground, the end of the keen blade pointing towards one of the many footpaths. The boy picked it up, and it tumbled from his hand again, pointing in the same direction. He picked it up the second time, and again the knife fell from his hand and pointed to the footpath. For the third time he lifted the knife from the ground, and as it fell no more, he placed it in his wallet, and went on his way.

"Thus he continued for many hours. When he was in doubt about the way, Keen-Point would show him. When he grew hungry, he ate the food his mother had placed in his wallet. It was late in the day when he started, and before he came to the spring and the pomegranate-tree, the sun went down and night came on. The boy stopped under a wide-spreading tree, said his prayers, placed his wallet under his head for a pillow, and went to sleep.

"'Bright and early the next morning he was up and going. Whenever he had any doubt about the way, Keen-Point would show him, and before the sun was up very high, he came in sight of the pomegranate-tree, with its red and golden fruit, and he knew the spring was close by.

"As he went on he grew thirstier, and thirstier, and when he came to where the cool, clear waters of the spring were bubbling from the ground with a sort of gurgling sound, his throat and mouth seemed to be as dry as paper. More than that, when he came to the spring, a traveler was sitting on one of the stones that lay around, drinking the water from a silver cup and peeling the rind from a pomegranate with a silver knife. The traveler had a very pleasant face and manner, and he spoke to the boy in the kindest way.

" ' If you want some water,' he said, ' you may drink from my silver cup. If you are hungry, you may peel a pomegranate with my silver knife.'

" The boy thanked the traveler and said that he would eat and drink later in the day. He thought to himself that a man who could drink from a silver cup and eat with a silver knife ought to be able to travel in a carriage or on horseback, but there was no horse nor carriage in sight.

" ' Well,' said the traveler, ' if you will neither eat nor drink, you can at least rest yourself.'

" So the boy seated himself on one of the big rocks close by the spring, and the traveler began to ask him all sorts of questions. What was his name, and where did he come from, and where was he going."

" What *was* his name ? " asked Sweetest Susan suddenly.

" Well, I declare ! " exclaimed Mrs. Meadows, " have n't I told you his name ? "

" If you did, we did n't hear you," said Buster John.

Mrs. Meadows raised her hands above her head

and let them fall helplessly in her lap. "I told you I didn't know how to tell stories!" she cried. "You had fair warning. Well, well, well! And I never even told you his name!" She paused and stared at the children as if she wanted them to pity her weakness. "To think that I should forget to call his name! Everybody knew it in my day and time, and they knew about his wonderful adventures.

"His name was Valentine, because he was born on St. Valentine's Day, and the little girl's name was Geraldine.

"Well, the traveler asked Valentine all sorts of questions, and tried hard to persuade him to drink some of the water and eat the pomegranate-seed.

"'I have heard,' said the traveler, 'that all this country around here is ruled by a cruel Conjurer, and that he has power over all except those who may chance to find this spring and this pomegranate-tree in passing, and drink of the water and eat of the fruit.'

"But Valentine shook his head. He said he would rather have milk than water any day, and as for pomegranates, he had no taste for them.

" 'Then I would advise you to go no farther,' said the traveler. 'If you fall into the hands of the Conjurer, you will never escape.'

" 'I have heard of this great Conjurer,' replied Valentine, 'and I should like nothing better than to see him.'

" He took Keen-Point from his wallet and pretended to be playing with it, letting it fall and picking it up. The knife pointed beyond the spring and the pomegranate-tree, and in a little while Valentine went on his journey. On the hill beyond the spring, he turned and looked back, but the traveler had disappeared. As there was no place where he could hide, Valentine concluded that the man he had seen was no traveler at all, but Rimrak, the Conjurer.

" But he was not afraid. He went on his way, and, after a little, came to a grove of the tallest and biggest trees he had ever seen. As he was passing through this grove, he suddenly saw two tremendous spiders running about among the trees before and behind him. Their bodies were as big as a feather bed when it is rolled up, and they were pretty much the same color. Valentine watched their antics a few minutes, and soon saw they were spinning a web among the trees and that he was in the middle of it.

"The big spiders ran about on the ground spinning their webs around him, and then they began to jump from tree to tree. Valentine began to have a creepy feeling up and down his back, for he didn't relish the idea of being caught in a spider's web like a bluebottle fly. He wondered why Cob-Handle hadn't warned him of the danger, and then he remembered that the case-knife was wrapped so tightly in his wallet that it couldn't give a warning if it was to try. So he took all the knives from the wallet, — Keen-Point, Cob-Handle, and Butch, — and placed them in his girdle.

"Valentine hardly had time to fasten the straps about the wallet, before he felt Cob-Handle jumping about and thumping against his side. Then he saw one of the big spiders coming towards him. Big as it was it moved nimbly, and before Valentine had time to get out of the way, it ran around him and wrapped a strand of its web about his legs. The strand was as big as a stout twine and as strong and as hard as wire. Then the big spider turned and came back, but by this time Valentine had drawn Butch from his belt, and as the ugly creature came near he struck at it with the knife, and cut off one of its hairy legs. The creature was so full of life and venom that its leg jumped around and clawed the ground for some little time.

"Holding Butch point down and edge outwards, Valentine cut the strand of web that held his legs. It was so large, and drawn so tightly about him, that it sounded like somebody had broken a fiddle-string. In this way he cut his way through the web. The crippled spider ran to his mate, and the two stood watching Valentine, their eyes shining green and venomous, and their jaws working as if they were chewing something."

"They were sharpening their teeth," Buster John suggested.

"I reckon so," replied Mrs. Meadows. "Anyhow they were ugly enough to scare anybody. Valentine cut his way through the web and marched out on the other side. He rested a little and then went on his way; but he had not gone far before Cob-Handle began to jump and thump

against his side. He stopped and looked around, but he could see nothing. He listened, but he could hear nothing.

" Presently he felt the ground moving beneath his feet, and he ran forward as fast as he could. And he did n't run too fast, either, for no sooner had he jumped away than a great hole appeared right where he had been standing. He could see that it was both wide and deep, but he did n't go back to look at it.

" No ; he kept on his way, and it was n't long before Cob-Handle began to jump and thump. Keen-Point also began to jump and thump, and showed him which way to go, and he ran as fast as he could. He heard a roaring sound as he started, and he had hardly got fifty steps away, though he was running with all his might, before a tremendous whirlwind came along, tearing up the bushes by roots and ploughing the ground. It came so close to Valentine that if he had had on a long-tail coat, I believe it would have been tangled in the whirlwind.

" I tell you," Mrs. Meadows went on, seeing the children smiling, " it was no laughing matter to Valentine. He shivered and trembled

when he thought what a narrow escape he had
had.

"He went on his way, and in a little while
Cob-Handle began to jump and thump again.
Valentine, thus warned, stood still and looked
around more carefully than he had yet done.
Some distance off, he saw a horrible creature coming towards him. It was in the shape of a man,
but it had four arms and hands, and in each hand
it was flourishing a club. Its hair stood out from
its head like the shucks in a scouring-mop, and
as it came nearer, Valentine saw that it had three
eyes. — one on each side of its nose, and one in
its forehead.

"Keen-Point said, 'Go straight forward,' and
then Butch began to jump and thump, so Valentine placed Cob-Handle and Keen-Point in his
girdle, and took Butch in his hand. Holding the
point straight before him, he went towards the
misshapen creature. Its red and watery eyes were
blinking and winking, and its arms were thresh-
ing the air with the clubs at such a tremendous
rate that Valentine thought his hour had surely
come. But he shut his eyes and went straight at
the creature. The sharp point of Butch had no

sooner touched the monster on its hairy breast
than its hands dropped the clubs, and it ran howling back the way it came.

"Valentine followed fast enough to see the
creature enter a cave, and to this, Keen-Point
told him he must go. As he went forward, a
fierce-looking man came from the cave and stood
guarding the entrance. He was covered from
head to foot with silver armor, and he brandished
a long keen sword with a silver handle. But
Valentine went straight forward, holding Butch
in his hand. The long sword never touched him,
nor did the silver armor stand in his way. With
one blow against Butch the long sword was shat-
tered, and the silver armor fell away from Rimrak
like the hulls from a ripe hickory-nut. Rimrak
himself fell before Butch and disappeared with
a hissing sound; and then the cave was no longer
dark. Its roof seemed to roll away; and where
the cave had been, there stood a great company
of people who had been held captive by the Conjurer. They stood wondering what had happened
and what would happen next. Among them was
Geraldine. She knew Valentine, and ran to him,
and then he was very happy. The people whom

he had rescued, gathered around him and thanked him and thanked him ; and some would have rewarded him, but he said he deserved none. He had come after the little girl, and he was not responsible for any accidents that happened to other people. This is what he said, and this is how he felt; but the people wondered that a young boy should be so bold and yet so modest.

"So they talked together, and decided to go with him to his home. Their horses and their carriages they found in good order, and in a little while they formed a procession. In this way they carried Valentine to his home, crying out to the people they passed, —

"'This is our deliverer! This is the brave boy that conquered Rimrak, the great Conjurer!'

"They carried Valentine to his home, and then they went with him to Geraldine's home. There was great rejoicing in the town. The little girl's father was rich, and he called all the people together, and they had a big dinner, and everybody was happy. The little girl had her old nurse back, and she grew up to be a beautiful young woman, and Valentine grew up to be a handsome young man."

XIX.

"I THINK that was a beautiful story," said Sweetest Susan, when Mrs. Meadows paused; " but was that the end?"

"Why, was n't that enough?" inquired Mr. Rabbit sleepily. "What more could you ask? Did n't the boy and girl get back home where they could get something to eat?"

"What became of them?" asked Buster John. "The stories about boys and girls in books say they married and lived happily ever after."

"Oh, yes!" cried Mr. Thimblefinger. "I 've heard about it. I remember the poetry, —

> "' They married, then, and lived in clover,
> And when they died, they died all over.'"

"Well," said Mrs. Meadows, " I thought surely you 'd get tired of Valentine and Geraldine by the time they got back home, and so I thought we 'd do well to leave them there. Still, if you are not tired —" Mrs. Meadows paused and looked at the children.

" Oh, we are not tired," protested Buster John.

" Well," said Mrs. Meadows, " if that's the case, I'll tell you what happened after Valentine and Geraldine went back home. Of course, Geraldine's father and mother were very proud and happy when their little girl was brought back to them. They were very grateful to Valentine, and they offered him money. But somehow Valentine didn't want their money. He said that the pleasure of getting Geraldine out of the hands of the wicked Conjurer was reward enough for him, and so he shook his head and refused the money that was offered him.

" Now, the little girl's father was rich and prosperous, while Valentine was very poor, and it was natural that the rich man should wonder why the boy, who was poor, should refuse money. Somehow, he took a dislike to Valentine. He said to himself that a boy who would refuse money as a free gift would never be prosperous.

" As time went on, Valentine grew to be a handsome young man, but he was still poor. He went to see Geraldine sometimes, but as she grew

older, she grew shyer. Valentine could n't understand this, but he thought it was because she was
old enough to know that she was rich and he
was poor.

"He said to her one day. 'You are not as
friendly as you used to be.'

"'Oh, yes I am,' she replied. 'I shall always
be friendly with you.'

"'No,' said he, 'you have changed.'

"'No more than you,' was her answer.

"'I changed?' he cried. 'I love you more
than I ever did.'

"With that Geraldine hung her head to
hide her blushes, but Valentine thought she was
angry. He turned on his heel and would have
gone away, but she called him back, and told him
not to go away angry — and then they made it up
somehow. Valentine said he would speak to Geraldine's father. This he did, but the father
shook his head.

"'You want to take her to a hut?' he cried.
'Why she might as well have stayed in the Conjurer's cave. Go and get you a fortune, and then
come back, and maybe we 'll talk the matter over.'

"Valentine went away very sad. He never

turned his head, although Geraldine was watching him from a window, ready to wave her hand and throw him a kiss. He wandered off into the woods until he came to the bank of the River, and there he sat watching the water go by. He watched it until he almost forgot his own trouble. It went along slowly and majestically, and sometimes it seemed to come eddying back to kiss the bank at his feet. For a little while it smoothed the wrinkles in his mind. He wondered where the River came from and where it was going to. It was always coming and always going, and there was never an end to it. All day long it went by, sometimes laughing and playing in the shallows and sometimes sighing a little under the willows.

" Valentine watched it and listened to the pleasant sounds it made until he began to feel as if the River was something like a friend and companion. It soothed his grief and drove away his loneliness. Being alone, he began to speak his thoughts aloud.

" ' Oh ! I wish I had a friend as strong and as powerful as the River ! ' he cried.

" ' And why not ? ' he heard a voice say. The water at his feet splashed a little louder. He looked around, but saw no one; he listened, but heard nothing.

"'I wonder who could have spoken?' he said aloud.

"'Who but your friend, the River?' a Voice replied.

"'Please don't mock me, whoever you are. There is no fun in misfortune,' said Valentine.

"'None at all,' responded the Voice. 'I am your friend the River. I will give you all the aid in my power.'

"'How am I to know the River is talking?' Valentine asked.

"'By this,' replied the River. At the word, a wave larger than all the rest sprang up the bank, and threw its spray in Valentine's hair and face. 'That is my salute,' said the River. 'It is a rough way, but I know no other. Now, how can I aid you?'

"'That is what troubles me,' responded Valentine. 'You are always going; you never stay.'

"'True,' said the River; 'but I am always coming. Therefore I must be always returning.'

"'But how?' Valentine asked.

"'Not this way,' said the River, 'but over

your head. When in the early morning, or in the warmer noon, or in the pleasant evenings, you see the white clouds flying westward, you may be sure that I am returning.' Then the River broke into a thousand ripples, as if smiling.

"But Valentine sat with a very serious face. 'I do not know how you can aid me,' he sighed.

"'I know what you wish,' the River replied. 'You wish riches.'

"'Yes,' said Valentine, 'but not for the sake of the riches themselves.'

"'Of course not!' the River exclaimed. 'Riches would be worthless if they could not command something better; and they are worse than worthless when the power they give is used for evil. I can give you riches, but not without your help. I can give you the power to obtain wealth, but I cannot give you the power to use it as it should be used.'

"Valentine listened to the mysterious Voice of the River like one in a dream. He could hardly believe his ears.

"'You say nothing,' said the River; 'you seem half asleep. But if I am to help you, you must help yourself. Walk by my side a little way.

Further down you will come to a boat that has drifted against the bank.'

" Valentine rose and stretched himself, and walked by the side of the River. He had not gone far before he came upon a boat that had drifted into an eddy. It lay there rocking, and a long oar rested against the seat.

" 'Jump in,' said the River; 'shove the boat away from the bank and trust to me. Take the oar and pull, and I will push you along.'

" Valentine did as he was told, and he soon found that the boat was gliding swiftly along. The trees and houses on each side seemed to be running a race to the rear, and the boats that he passed on the River seemed to be standing still. He went on for some hours, always trusting to the River. When he grew tired, he held his oar in the air and rested, but whether he rested or whether he rowed, he saw that his boat was always gliding swiftly along.

" Presently, in the far distance, he could see the spires and steeples of a city, and he wondered whether he would be compelled to go gliding by, or whether the River would land him there. But he was not left long in doubt.

"'That is your future home,' said the River. 'There you will find friends, and there you will become rich and famous.'

"'But how?' asked Valentine.

"'I can only tell you the beginning,' replied the River. 'When your boat glides to the landing-place, you will see there an old gentleman richly dressed. He will ask you if you have seen his little son. He has been there every day for two days, and he has asked of all comers the same question.'

"'What shall I say to him?' asked Valentine.

"'Tell him you have not seen his son,' replied the River, 'but that you feel sure you can find the boy. Tell the old gentleman that you have come a long journey, and need rest, but that when you have refreshed yourself, you will go and seek his son.'

"'But where shall I seek for the boy?' asked Valentine.

"'Come to me,' said the River. 'I will be here. I am always going, and yet I am always coming.'

"By this time they had come to the city. 'Row for the landing,' said the River; 'your fortune is there.'

"Valentine dipped his oar in the water and rowed to the landing. He leaped from his boat, threw the chain around a stake, and looked around. Sure enough, an old gentleman, richly dressed, was walking up and down, his hands crossed behind him. When he saw Valentine he paused and looked at him. Valentine bowed politely as he had been taught to do.

"'You are a comely lad,' said the old gentleman. 'Did you come down the River, or from below?'

"'I came down the River,' replied Valentine, touching his hat again.

"'I have lost my youngest son,' said the old gentleman. 'He is a little boy about six years old. He wandered from home two days ago, came to the River landing, and was last seen playing in a boat. I have been trying to find him. My boats have been searching in all directions, but the child cannot be found.'

"'I think I can find him,' said Valentine, 'but first I must rest and refresh myself. I have come a long journey, and I am tired.'

"The old gentleman seized him by the hand. 'Come with me!' he exclaimed. 'You shall go to my house. Your every want shall be supplied. If you succeed in finding my lost boy you shall have whatever you ask for.'

" 'I shall ask for nothing,' replied Valentine. 'The pleasure I shall have in restoring your son to your arms will be sufficient reward for me.'

" ' Nevertheless,' said the gentleman, ' you shall have a more substantial reward than that.'

" So he took Valentine home, and treated him with the greatest kindness. He was served with rich food and the finest spiced wines, and fitted out with an elegant suit of clothes. Early the next morning, Valentine thanked the gentleman for his kindness.

" 'I go now,' he said, ' to find your son. Watch for me near the River. I may return soon, or I may be gone long, but when I return I will bring your son.'

" 'You are young,' remarked the gentleman. ' You are hopeful and brave. You imagine you can succeed where others have failed. But I fear not. My lost boy has been sought by men older than you, and quite as brave, but they have not found him.'

" 'Certainly, I may fail,' Valentine replied.

'If I depended on myself alone, I know I would fail. But I trust in Providence.'

"Valentine and the gentleman then went to the River — one to go in search of the lost child, and the other to watch and wait for the return. Valentine went to the water's edge.

"'Get a boat with a sail,' whispered the River, lapping the sand at his feet. This was provided at once, for the gentleman was very wealthy, and then Valentine set out on his voyage. 'Go back the way you came,' said the River, 'but keep out of the middle current. Let the wind fill your sails and carry you near the shore, on the right.' With the River to direct him, Valentine sailed along with a light heart and a happy mind. For more than two hours he journeyed up the River, and it was not until the sun was low in the west that the River told him to lower the sails of his boat. This done, the River carried his boat gently ashore, and as it glided on the sand. he saw, near by, a boat, in which a little boy lay fast asleep. Without disturbing him, Valentine lifted the little fellow in his arms, and transferred him to the new boat, in which wraps, and cloaks, and food had been placed.

"It was easy to guess how the little boy had been lost. He had gone to play in a boat, which broke loose from its fastenings, and drifted slowly up the River in the eddies that play hide and seek near the bank. The first day the searchers searched for him, they went too far. The next day they searched too near, and so the child drifted and drifted, and was lost sure enough. He was very cold and wet when Valentine found him, but in a little while he was warmly wrapped in the cloaks that had been provided.

"'Take his boat in tow,' said the River. 'Let your sails stay down, and take the oars and row home as hard as you can.'

"The River helped with its swift current, and it was not long before Valentine caught a glimpse of the bonfire that was burning at the landing to light him back to the city.

"There was great rejoicing when Valentine returned with the lost child. The bells were rung and salutes fired from the big cannon that commanded the approaches to the city. It turned out that the gentleman whose child Valentine had found was the ruler of the city, and you may depend upon it he was grateful to the unknown young man.

" But in all large cities there are some envious people, and these soon had it whispered about that Valentine was a mere adventurer who had stolen the child and hid it so that he might rescue it again when a big reward was offered. These whispers grew thicker and thicker until at last they reached the ears of every one. No one knew Valentine, and appearances were against him, but one day he was approached by an old man with a long white beard, who asked him from whence he came. The old man was so kind and agreeable in his manner that Valentine told him the story of the rescue of Geraldine.

"Much to his surprise the old man rose and embraced him. ' Come with me !' he cried. So saying, he carried Valentine to the market-place, and there in the presence of a great crowd of people, the old man said : —

"' Behold my rescuer ! Behold the brave youth who conquered Rimrak, the Conjurer.'

" This closed the mouths of the envious, and when that happens, there is not much more to tell in any story."

Here Mrs. Meadows paused and looked at Mr. Rabbit, who sat fast asleep in his chair.

"Did he get rich and marry Geraldine?" inquired Sweetest Susan.

"Why of course," replied Mrs. Meadows. "Do you reckon he'd have gone through all these ups and downs if he was n't to marry and settle down and be happy in the end?"

"Well," said Buster John, "it was a pretty good story."

"I speck so," remarked Drusilla, "but dey's lots too much richness in it fer me."

Mrs. Meadows laughed so heartily at this that Mr. Rabbit was aroused from his nap, and looked around in surprise.

"Did I hear somebody say supper was ready?" he asked.

Mrs. Meadows laughed again, but this time she glanced at the sky of Mr. Thimblefinger's queer country. It had grown perceptibly darker. Mr. Thimblefinger drew out his little watch. Mr. Rabbit closed one eye, and sat as if listening for something.

"Well," said Mrs. Meadows with a sigh, "I reckon we'll have to tell you good-by for this time, but I do hope you'll come again. I declare it has been a treat to have some new somebody to

talk to. By the time you get back home the sun will be setting in your country, and your folks will begin to be uneasy about you."

The children were not at all anxious to go. They had had a very curious experience in Mr. Thimblefinger's queer country, and they had almost forgotten that the sun in their part of the world had a habit of going down. But they said they were ready, and then they shook hands all around. When Buster John came to shake hands with Mr. Rabbit, the latter looked at the youngster a moment.

" Did you ever happen to know a colored man named Aaron ? " he asked.

" Uncle Aaron ! " exclaimed Buster John. " Why, he lives on our plantation. He's the foreman."

" Well," said Mr. Rabbit solemnly, " when you see Aaron, take his left hand in both of yours, bend his thumb back a little, and with your right thumb make this mark ✻. The first time he will pay no attention. Make it the second time. Then he will be ready to listen. Make it the third time. Then he will ask you what you want. Say to him that you want to learn the language of the animals."

" Won't he get angry ? " asked Buster John.

" Try him," replied Mr. Rabbit with a cunning look. " Now, good-by ! "

" When you get ready to come again," said Mrs. Meadows, " just drop a big apple in the spring, and I'll be bound we'll all see it and know what it means. And when you come be sure and bring the apple. It's been a month of Sundays since I've had one."

The children promised they would, and then, with Mr. Thimblefinger leading the way, they started home, which they reached without further adventure. As they stood on the brink of the spring, waving their hands to Mr. Thimblefinger, who was smiling at them from the bottom, Drusilla remarked with unction : —

" I dunner how 't is wid you all, but I don't no mo' b'lieve we been down dar under dat water dar dan — dan — dan de man in de moon. Dat I don't ! "

Then the youngsters heard the supper-bell ring, and they all ran towards the house.